HER DARING EARL
AN ENEMIES-TO-LOVERS REGENCY ROMANCE

NOBLE PURSUITS
BOOK TWO

ELLIE ST. CLAIR

♥ **Copyright 2024 Ellie St Clair**

All rights reserved.

This book or parts thereof may not be reproduced in any form, stored in any retrieval system, or transmitted in any form by any means—electronic, mechanical, photocopy, recording, or otherwise—without prior written permission of the publisher.

Facebook: Ellie St. Clair

Cover by AJF Designs

Do you love historical romance? Receive access to a free ebook, as well as exclusive content such as giveaways, contests, freebies and advance notice of pre-orders through my mailing list!

Sign up here!

A trigger warning for this book can be found here. Please note that it will give away elements of the plot. https://elliestclair.com/trigger-warnings

Noble Pursuits
Her Runaway Duke
Her Daring Earl
Her Honorable Viscount

For a full list of all of Ellie's books, please see
www.elliestclair.com/books.

CHAPTER 1

It was an impossible task.

Marrying off all seven of his sisters?

Sisters who, while all intriguing in their own way, were not exactly what most men of the *ton* would consider marriage material?

It would take a miracle.

Fitz watched them as they danced together in one corner of the ballroom. Well, five of them. Two of them were not yet old enough to attend such events.

Thank goodness.

He could barely handle the first five.

"Having a good time?"

Fitz turned at the voice, his smile breaking free when he recognized his long-time friend, Baxter Munroe. The man had very few flaws but for an inescapable one – his sister.

Some might argue that his generous mustache was also suspect, but Fitz appreciated the way it flourished and how Munroe wore it without shame.

"I will have a much better time once my mother takes my sisters home," Fitz said, running a hand through his hair, unable to help the self-deprecating laugh that escaped. The duty of his sisters should cause him a great deal of consternation, but he couldn't allow his thoughts about it to deepen, or he would never be able to focus on anything else.

"They're a lively lot," Munroe said, taking a sip of his drink as he watched the girls. They should be standing demurely on the side of the dance floor, waiting to be asked for a dance or a turn about the room. But no. Not Fitz's sisters. Instead, they were moving back and forth in time to the music, dancing with one another, unable to quietly wait – except for Sloane, who looked about ready to fall asleep.

"They're not unlike you," Munroe commented, viewing Fitz from the corner of his eyes.

"What's that supposed to mean?" Fitz asked, although he was already chuckling, knowing exactly what it meant. He was also not one to wait around idly.

Munroe only shook his head. "Thank goodness I've only one sister to marry off – and my father is still around to worry about her."

That shortened Fitz's laugh. He didn't want to think about Baxter's sister. She caused him more consternation than his own.

"Why is your mother in such a hurry suddenly?" Munroe asked. "What has changed?"

"Dot is four and twenty. Far older than young women should be to be married, at least according to my mother. All Dot wants to do, unfortunately, is become a midwife. Can you believe such a thing? My mother is beside herself and refuses to allow her to do such common work. Of course, Dot has a mind of her own, and you can hardly barricade a woman her age in her bedchamber, so my mother has tasked me with finding someone for her – and the others who are old enough."

"You have quite the job ahead of you."

"Don't I know it? I've practically begged half of the men here to dance with them, but I've heard every excuse there is as to why they cannot. Lost all humility I ever had to begin with."

Munroe laughed long and loud as Fitz finally sighed, shaking his head. "My parents really should have ensured that my sisters attended all of their dance lessons instead of the other pursuits they busied themselves with. Now they cannot find a dance partner due to all of these men who fear having their toes stepped on."

"Well, lucky for you, Fitz, I am a brave man."

Fitz looked up at Munroe with more hope than he should have dared felt. "You'll dance with them?"

"One of them," Munroe said, holding up an index finger as a slight look of horror flashed over his face. "Do not get too excited."

"One is wonderful," Fitz said, effusively taking Munroe's drink out of his hand and setting it down before he could change his mind. He led Munroe to where Dot, Henrietta, Sloane, Georgina, and Sarah waited. "Start with Dot."

"Start? I just said—"

"Here we are. Dot, Lord Anderson here has a question for you."

Baxter shot him a quick look that was part disdain, part amusement before reaching out and taking Dot's hand, bowing low.

"Lady Dot, would you permit me a dance?"

Dot, with her usual matter-of-fact expression affixed to her, looked at first Munroe and then Fitz with skepticism before nodding her head. "Very well. It will appease Mother."

Munroe appeared flummoxed, unable to articulate a response as he led her out onto the dance floor, where couples were gathering for the next set. He leaned in as he passed Fitz. "Favor for a favor, Fitz. Find my sister."

Fitz closed his eyes for a moment, wondering if he could pretend that he didn't hear Munroe's request. But the man had a point. If he didn't return the favor, how could he ever ask Munroe for anything again?

He reluctantly turned around to look for her.

Only to find her standing behind him, her arms crossed and a jaunty smile on her face as though she was expecting him and knew exactly what he was thinking.

A terrifying thought, indeed.

* * *

"LADY ELIZA." Fitz drew a visible intake of breath before forcing a smile for her.

Of all the men in all of London, it had to be him. Here. Now. If she'd had time once she realized it was him standing in front of her, she would have backed away before he had noticed her. She had allowed her intrigue in the interaction between her brother and Dot to distract her. "Lovely to see you."

"Oh, Fitz." She rolled her eyes, knowing he would never have noticed her had she not been standing so close. He had made his disinterest abundantly clear years ago. "Don't do that. Not to me."

"I am sure that I do not know what you are talking about," he said smartly, rocking back and forth on his heels.

"Drop the act, Fitz."

He eyed her momentarily before his lips curled up into his signature smile and his heels dropped onto the ground. "Very well. Lady Eliza, it has not been long enough since we last saw one another. I am sorry that we are meeting again."

"There, was that so hard?" She practically beamed, even though her feet were telling her to run as fast as she could away from this man. Other parts of her were saying something else, which was precisely the problem, and why she had no business being anywhere near him.

"Eliza!" Henrietta gasped from beside her, but Hen didn't

understand. She never had. She loved her brother, and rightly so. Eliza was sure that Fitz was a wonderful brother to his seven sisters, two of whom – twins, Henrietta and Sloane – were close friends of hers. But he wasn't Eliza's brother. Not by a long shot. And he wasn't so wonderful to her.

"Would you like to dance?" he asked, the question clearly painful for him to muster.

"No," she answered honestly. She had another goal in mind tonight. She was on the hunt. Not for a husband, but something else entirely. "But if I deny you with my mother and the rest of the *ton* looking on, then there is sure to be, at the very least, scandal, and far more likely and annoying, my mother will pester me to know why I would turn down a man who is such close friends with our family and who has been so supportive of us. I do hate to disappoint my mother after all she has done for me."

"You are such a wonderful daughter."

"Do not patronize me."

"Very well," he said, lifting his brows. "But you do realize that you could have been like every other woman who is asked to dance by a man she despises and simply said yes."

"Where is the fun in that? Besides, I'm not doing this for you. I'm doing it for my brother. He needs to make it look as though he is doing his duty in trying to marry me off and he thinks by asking you to return his favor and dance with me, it will be good enough."

"Must you be so forthright?"

"I must."

"What has gotten into you two?" Henrietta asked, looking between Eliza and her brother. "Dance or not but please do not subject me to such tension."

"Very well. My apologies, Hen," Eliza said as she reached out and practically snatched Fitz's arm. He said nothing as he led her to the middle of the floor where the musicians had just struck up a waltz. Of course. It had to be a waltz. One of his arms came around her, the other took her hand in his.

"It's been a while since we danced," he murmured against her ear, his breath hot on her neck. Eliza hated herself for the involuntary shiver he evoked within her. It was the kind of shiver she was looking for, but not from Fitz.

"Not long enough," she countered as stoutly as she could, becoming even more annoyed when he ignored her.

"I do not believe I have seen you since we were both at Greystone with Siena and Levi. What a time that was."

"It most certainly was," she said, wondering if it was the first time they had agreed on something.

"I hope you noticed how well-behaved I was during our time there."

"What does it matter what I think?" She furrowed her brow and leaned away from him so she could see into his face. "Besides, I am sure it must have been difficult for you to go so long without a woman warming your bed."

A smirk began to play over his lips and Eliza knew him well enough to be aware that a joke had come to him, one that she would likely rather not hear.

Finally, he couldn't help himself.

"It must have been difficult for you to resist volunteering for the job."

"I would rather sleep in the barn."

Then he did something that surprised her more than she would like.

He threw back his head and laughed out loud.

His laugh was one of those that was so overwhelmingly contagious, loud and booming, that all of the couples nearby and even those close to the other side of the dance floor turned toward them in both shock and interest to see what had so enraptured the earl.

Eliza lifted her hand off of his shoulder ever so slightly and smacked him. "Stop that."

"Why? You made the joke!"

"Everyone is staring."

"Do you care?" he asked, lifting a brow, and not for the first time, Eliza cursed him for how handsome he was.

"I do not. But my mother will. And your mother will. And then there will be hell to pay after this."

"I am a grown man, two and thirty. An earl. It doesn't matter what my mother thinks."

"Does it not?" Eliza said, lifting a brow and taking a small step backward. "Perhaps, then, we should go find her to discuss your intentions on taking a bride. I am sure she has an opinion. In fact—"

"You will do no such thing," he practically growled, pulling her so quickly and tightly against him that she gasped, feeling every hard muscle not otherwise cloaked in an abundance of fabric meld against her body. "My mother does not need to know of such things."

"Because you are scared of her," she teased.

"I am not."

"You are! Otherwise, you wouldn't pay her interest in marrying off your sisters any mind and you would let Dot do exactly what she wants to do."

"And be a midwife?"

"She loves it."

"Just as I love new adventures. But you are not going to find me traipsing around the countryside night and day to fulfill my dreams. I have a job to do, and I am not going to shirk it. Dot also needs to do what she must."

"Says who?"

"Says…" he blinked, and she knew she had him for a moment. He shook his head abruptly. "Society. My mother. My father."

"Your father is dead, so he doesn't care. Your mother will be fine, and in fact, it seems to me she rather likes having her daughters nearby. She just thinks it is proper to marry them off. And you only care about society because of your political ambitions."

"I am an earl. I have my seat regardless of what people think of me."

She narrowed her eyes at him. "I know you. You want people to think that you have no cares in the world, but you want them to respect you so that they listen to what you say and put credence in your opinions."

He leaned in toward her, more eagerness in his stance than she had ever seen in him before. He was usually such a carefree, lackadaisical man. "I want to create change, Eliza. To do that, I need people to support me."

"What kind of change?" she asked, suddenly intrigued, even though the song was beginning to come to a close.

"What the hell?" he growled, causing Eliza to start.

"That is not exactly the language—"

But he had dropped his arms and left her, already walking away without another word.

"What in the world?" she muttered, knowing she should leave this be. She was here tonight to find a man who would teach her all that she had longed to know but never experienced. She should focus on her own goals.

She was unable to help her curiosity, however, as she followed Fitz across the dance floor in time to see him stop in front of Dot, whose hand was caught in that of a tall, thin man – Lord Mandrake if she was not mistaken.

"Mandrake!" Fitz practically bellowed, causing Eliza to jump. He was not usually a man with a temper, at least as far as she knew – and she knew him better than she would like.

"Get your hands off my sister!"

CHAPTER 2

"Fitz." Mandrake turned around with a slow, brittle smile growing on his slender lips. "Just the man I want to see."

"It's *Lord Fitzroy*," Fitz ground out from between his clenched teeth. "Only my friends call me Fitz."

Mandrake's smile didn't falter, which only further enraged Fitz. It was so phony, he hoped that Dot could see right through it as well.

"Hopefully in time then."

Fitz stared at him, aware that his initial outburst had caused many eyes to turn his way.

"Fitz," Dot said from between clenched teeth, "is there a problem?"

"You will not dance with this man."

"Lord Mandrake has not even asked me to dance yet."

"I was about to," Mandrake said more smoothly than Fitz would have liked. "In fact, I would like to ask for more than that."

"Mandrake—"

"I would like permission to call upon your sister. Tomorrow, if that would be all right with you, Lady Dot."

"I—" Dot looked from him and back to Fitz, who was about to step between them. "I think perhaps we should have this conversation somewhere else. Not with all of these eyes upon us."

Why did his sister have to be so damn level-headed?

"Fine," Fitz said in a low voice. "You can come to my townhouse tomorrow. But to talk to me. Not to Dot. Understood?"

"Very well," Lord Mandrake said. "I look forward to seeing you again, Lady Dot."

"Goodnight."

Mandrake began to walk away but Fitz sensed motion behind him, and he turned around to find that Eliza was still standing there, her eyes wide as she had apparently witnessed the entire exchange. Damn it.

"Lady Eliza," Mandrake said, stopping in front of her and lifting her hand to his lips, placing a kiss upon it. Her eyes grew, the blue of them becoming even more vivid. Fitz's ire flared, although this time, he couldn't do anything about it. He had no say over Eliza. But her brother did. He looked around, trying to find Baxter, hoping he could come and put a stop to this, but Baxter was nowhere in sight. Typical.

"Move along, Mandrake," Fitz droned loudly instead, causing both Eliza and his sister to gape at him. Damn it again.

Mandrake smirked at him knowingly before finally doing as Fitz requested, leaving him alone.

Only, he wasn't alone. Not only were three of his sisters with him – he belatedly noticed Hen and Sloane standing there – but Eliza didn't appear to be going anywhere.

"What?" he huffed as he met their stares. "I can't stand that man."

"Whyever not?" Dot asked.

Fitz gaped at her. "Seriously? He is only trying to become close to you to annoy me!"

Dot crossed her arms over her chest. "I find that quite offensive, Fitz. And why do you care if he speaks to Eliza? Minutes ago, it appeared the two of you would have loved nothing more than to never speak with one another again."

Fitz shifted from one foot to the other.

"I was looking out for her on behalf of her brother."

Eliza rolled her eyes. "I think I have heard enough. I shall speak with you ladies later?"

At their nods, she turned and walked away, and Fitz couldn't help but watch her and the swish of her hips, wondering what she was going to do next. Who would she dance with? Why did he care?

When he turned back around, his sisters were all watching him closely – even Sloane, who usually hardly paid him any attention at all.

"What is going on between you and Eliza?" Henrietta asked, and Fitz shook his head.

"Nothing," he muttered. "Nothing at all."

"Doesn't seem like nothing," Dot remarked, and Fitz wondered why all of the women in his life were so inquisitive and could not just accept what he told them like most women of their station.

"I'm tired," Sloane said with a yawn as she reached her arms up over her head. "I'm going to find Mother."

"Not yet," Henrietta said, her usual smile turning into a pout. "I'm having such fun."

"You always are," Sloane said. "Besides, by the time Mother agrees to leave, you shall be ready."

"Very well," Henrietta agreed before fixing an eye on Fitz.

"I'm not sure what you've done with my lighthearted brother," she said. "But I'd like him back now, if you please."

*　*　*

IT WAS MUCH LATER than Fitz would have liked when he saw his mother and sisters home. He led them into the house before returning to the carriage, refusing to answer their questions about where he was going or who he was going to see – and why they couldn't go with him. It was time for him to have some fun of his own.

He knew what Eliza thought of him. That he was a rake, taking one woman after another without regard for their emotions. In that, however, she was wrong. He was a *flirt*, not a rake. He enjoyed the attention of ladies, but he didn't follow through to anything more with most of them. He liked to be liked and enjoyed a little friendly banter. What was the problem with that?

But if that's what she wanted to think of him, then he might as well live up to her expectations. Tonight, he would go see Madeline. She could provide easy company and comfort that he wasn't getting anywhere else, that was for certain.

He stepped out of his carriage, instructing his driver to return home. He would call for a hack later in the night. He pushed open the door of The Scarlet Rose, which was dimly lit by flickering candles glowing in front of red velvet walls. The tables were littered with discarded cards and empty glasses, the high ceilings adorned with chandeliers dripping with crystals, although Fitz doubted their authenticity.

The air was heavy with the scent of tobacco and alcohol mixed with a faint hint of sweat and desperation. A sweet yet suffocating aroma of expensive perfumes lingered through the corners of the room, all not so different from the ballroom he had just left.

The occasional cry of victory punctuated the room along with the forced laughter of the women who were paid to be there.

One of whom he set out to find.

He weaved his way through the gentlemen who were

throwing cards, many with women on their laps. He wasn't here for games. He actually wasn't much of a gambler – not with cards, anyway. He would rather take risks in other areas of his life. He would far prefer a dare of consequence, one that took him on an adventure that provided a true thrill, not a superficial one like the throw of a good card which served to fool most of the men in here.

"Madeline!" he exclaimed, a smile breaking out on his face when the dark-haired woman turned his way from her perch on a high stool in the corner of the hell – almost as though she was waiting for him.

A beauty mark that he was certain was added with charcoal sat above her red-painted lips, the rouge highlighting her cheekbones. He wasn't sure that she could be called beautiful, but she was certainly striking. He had been attracted to her in the past, but suddenly he found that her beauty was no longer quite so alluring. He was craving something far more natural. Softer. Less calculating.

Damn Eliza Munroe. Why was she in his head? She was his sisters' friend. Not a woman who he should be pursuing, especially after the… incident.

Yet he still enjoyed Madeline's company. She lived boldly, laughed loudly, and was never afraid to say things as they were.

"Fitz. I haven't seen you in ages but heard that you were back in London. I was hoping you would come by," she said, leaning over, holding her cigarette just beyond him as she lightly kissed his cheek. He had to fight the urge to wipe off her lipstick, even though he knew it was practically part of the accepted attire here.

"It has been a while," he said, leaning back, finding her perfume slightly too sweet. "I've been occupied."

"Ah yes, with your friend, the Duke of Death," she said, raising an eyebrow. "We hear just as much – if not more – in here as most do in your ballrooms."

"Likely more," he agreed, grimacing slightly when she mentioned Levi's nickname. He knew it was said all around London, and yet he didn't appreciate hearing it. "The Duke of *Dunmore*, however, is happier now than I have ever seen him, so it was well worth it."

"Good," she said, softening somewhat before looking around. "Would you like a moment alone?"

"I would," he said, straightening his spine, recalling his resolve. He was here for a purpose. To scratch the itch that had been bothering him for far too long. Since he had been away at Levi's. Had it truly been that long? He rubbed the back of his neck, which had begun to heat up as he tried to ignore just what – that was, *who* – had caused it.

"Come," she said, tilting her head toward the back of the room as she held out a hand. "We'll go to a private room."

He took her hand, following her, nodding to other gentlemen along the way who greeted him with knowing smiles, causing his shoulders to tighten. Since when had he cared so much about people knowing his business?

Since you began to care about what Eliza might think, said a little voice in his head – one that he tried to push away.

Madeline led them into one of the small back rooms, which Fitz imagined had been a bedroom at one point in time. It was draped in even more red velvet than the outside room, the bed sitting prominently in the middle.

She paused, staring at him for a moment with hesitation in her eyes. That was odd. "Drink?" she asked.

"Sure," he said, wiping his brow as sweat had begun to drip down. A drink would be most welcome. Should he not be looking forward to this? It certainly shouldn't be a chore.

She stood at the sideboard, her back to him, her long red dress nearly blending in with the wall in front of her.

"Whisky?" she said, her voice oddly detached.

"Whatever you have."

She turned around and when she passed him the glass, Fitz noticed that her hand was slightly shaking.

"Are you well?" he asked, narrowing his eyes for a better look at her, but she wouldn't meet his gaze.

"Fine."

"Are you certain?" he asked, and she nodded tersely.

He lifted the glass to his lips, about to take a sip when she whirled around, shocking him by lashing out, knocking the glass away so that the liquid sprayed all over the room.

"Madeline?" he gaped in astonishment as his hand remained outstretched in front of him, as though he was still about to bring the drink to his lips. "What in the—"

"You cannot drink that," she said with a shuddering breath. "It would kill you."

CHAPTER 3

Fitz continued to gawk in shock at the woman standing in front of him.

"It's whiskey," he said, finally regaining his composure as she stood in front of him, her chest heaving. "It might kill me eventually, but not today."

"No, it's not that." She shook her head. "It's poisoned."

"You poured it!" he couldn't help but exclaim, standing as he suddenly felt the need to take control of this situation.

"I know," she said, taking another shuddering breath as a tear leaked out of her eye and she quickly wiped it away, smearing the face paint beneath it. "I should never have been so tempted."

Fitz took a step forward, crossing his arms over his chest.

"I suggest you tell me the full story of what is happening."

"Very well," Madeline said, rocking back and forth from her heels to her toes. "I do not tell many people this, but I have a child. A daughter."

Fitz started in surprise. He had known her for some time and had never heard this before. "I see."

"I don't know who the father is. Don't worry, I had her long before I met you. I raised her myself and have no family.

I pay a woman to watch her while I am working, and it's a struggle."

"I can understand that," he said, sympathetic to her plight but still not understanding what that had to do with this strange situation.

"I was offered a great sum of money to poison your drink."

"By whom?" Fitz asked, astonished.

"I'm not sure. I wasn't asked directly. It was through a note left for me here at the hell with an advance and a promise of the rest once you were dead."

"You were going to *kill* me? I do hope you are jesting." Fitz began to pace back and forth across the small room, unsure of what to believe at the moment.

"It was a great sum of money," she said, having the courtesy to appear chagrined, at least. "It could take care of my daughter for the rest of her life. But in the end, I couldn't do it."

"How wonderful of you," he intoned, and she dipped her head.

"It was wrong to even consider it, I know. But at least now you know, Fitz, that someone wants you dead."

"Whatever for?" he said, lifting his arms out to the side.

"I have no idea," she said. "I know nothing of your life. But you best be watchful."

"Oh, not to worry," he said. "I will."

He just wasn't sure whether or not to believe this ridiculous story.

She stepped forward toward him, trailing her fingers down his chest seductively.

"Should we go back to where we were?"

"No!" he said, throwing her hand away from him. "I think it is best that you stay far away from me."

Truth be told, he had been forcing himself to follow through on anything with her. Every time she stepped close to him, all he could see was Eliza's face, which caused him no shortage of chagrin. For he should have nothing to do with the woman. He knew that with every bit of his rational thought, and yet, his body didn't seem to understand.

"I'm sorry, Fitz," Madeline said, her face breaking slightly, bringing him back to the present moment. "I never meant to—"

"Look," he said, holding a finger up toward her. "I'm not entirely sure what you want from me right now. A thank you for not killing me? I am glad that your conscience came through in the end, but at the moment, I am slightly more concerned with the fact that you were, for a time, willing to go through with my demise for a fee. Now, I am going to take my leave. I won't report you to anyone, for which you should be grateful as one word from me could ruin your life. I would not, however, do that to your daughter."

"Thank you," she said, her eyes brimming with tears. Fitz knew he was being hard on her, and understood her pain, and yet, he was more shaken than he'd like to admit that he had nearly died by her hands.

He shook his head as he flung open the door and walked out. Who would possibly want him dead? Yes, there could be political motives, but at this point, he had the *desire* to make change – he was not yet actually going through the motions to do so. No one would have any more reason to do away with him than any other member of the House of Lords.

Ridiculous.

As he pushed his way through the gaming hell part of the establishment, he avoided eye contact as best he could, not stopping but lifting his hand in greeting anytime he saw a familiar face. He didn't seem to have it within him to make jovial conversation at the moment. Not after the evening he'd had.

The only person he saw was Baxter, sitting near the exit,

watching the night's procedures with a smile beneath his mustache.

"Baxter," he nodded to him.

"Where are you off to?" Baxter asked. "I've just arrived."

"I've had enough fun for one night," Fitz grunted.

"What's that supposed to mean?"

"Ask Madeline. She's poisonous this evening. Literally."

With that, he stepped through the doors, the London air as crisp and as cool as could be, at least compared to the smoke and aromas that had been inside the hell. He lifted his hand, about to call for a hack, when he decided that the night was nice enough that a walk might clear his head.

He needed to shake loose the weight that had descended upon his shoulders, in the form of seven sisters who would need or soon need husbands, an earldom, his political goals, and a certain green-eyed woman his body refused to ignore.

And now there was this so-called plot to kill him.

He shook his head in disbelief, lifting his gaze to the sky, where the moon shone in a waxing crescent, stars surrounding it. It was so much clearer to view when he was out at his estate, but he seemed to be spending less and less time there as of late. It was hard to participate in politics and marry off sisters from the middle of Essex.

He was so caught up in his musings that he wasn't watching where he was going very carefully. Not that he needed to. The Scarlet Rose was on the edge of Soho, so it hadn't taken him long to cross over Regent Street and into Mayfair, where there was very little risk of being accosted by anyone dangerous. Perhaps the odd street urchin attempting to pick his pocket, but he could take one of the young lads if it came down to it.

Which is why he was caught off guard when he walked right into the man – and into something cold and hard that bit right through his jacket.

"Ow," he said, stepping back and rubbing his chest, staring up at the man in front of him.

Only he didn't just look up. He had to continue to crane his neck as the man stood towering above him.

"If you'll excuse me," Fitz said, attempting to step around him, and it was only then that he realized what he had initially missed in the dark – the object that had struck him in the chest had not done so accidentally. It was a pistol, held out in front of the man, pointed right at Fitz.

"I say," he said with a start. "What are you doing?"

"Keep walking," the man said, his voice low and nearly a grunt. "In between those buildings."

"I think not," Fitz said indignantly, aware that to do so would be signing his own death warrant. "I must say, I am becoming rather annoyed with these attempts on my life. Tell me, who sent you and what is he paying? I'll double it for his name."

He wasn't sure that he would actually be able to do so, but it was worth a try. Better to be without money and alive than in the ground with a fortune left behind above him.

"Can't do that or I'd be dead myself," the man said, shaking his head. "I have no other choice. Would have rather done this where it wouldn't make a mess."

As he slowly raised the pistol, Fitz looked around in some desperation. Surely there had to be some other lost soul wandering Mayfair at this time of night? This couldn't be the end. He still had much to do. Marry off seven sisters. Be a champion for change for those whose voices had been dimmed for far too long.

He only had one choice. He would have to rush the man.

He braced himself, ready to tackle him, knowing that he was likely to be hit by a stray bullet but willing to risk it. With a shout, he launched himself forward just as the man pulled the trigger.

* * *

"Well, that was a most interesting event," Eliza's mother said, rambling on as the carriage trundled down the road. Usually, Eliza was just as animated as her mother was in discussing an event they had just left, but tonight felt different.

And she knew exactly why.

Fitz.

Damn the man. The truth – one she had never shared with another person, not even Siena, her closest friend in the entire world – was that she had always had something of a penchant for him. It was not a sentiment of her choosing. It was as though her body was drawn to him on its own, despite all of her protestations that would have liked it to be otherwise.

Their dance had only made her confusion all the greater. It had reminded her of how frustrating he could be *and* further served to make her want him all the more.

They were like oil and water – made of the same state, but when they tried to mix, as close as they came to each other, they were always repelled away, unable to truly combine.

Maybe it would have been different, had he not done what he had.

But the past could not be changed, no matter how much she would like it to be, no matter how polite they had been to one another at Greystone. They had friends and family in common. That was it.

"Are you all right, darling?" her mother asked, finally realizing that her conversation had become a soliloquy.

"Fine," Eliza said, forcing a smile for her mother. She truly was the best mother Eliza could ever have asked for. She thought of Siena's parents and shuddered, knowing just what her life could have been like had she been born to others not so understanding. "I'm just tired."

"We did stay far too late, didn't we?" her mother said with a sigh. "Your father will be up waiting for us, wondering where we have gotten to."

Eliza's father preferred not to accompany them to such events unless it was an occasion of some importance that he would be expected to attend. He was far more of a bookish man, quiet and reserved – so unlike Eliza's mother. Yet, somehow, they were far better suited to one another than most couples of their station. They had made it work, which was all Eliza could ever ask for herself.

"I do wish I knew where Baxter had gotten to," her mother said, appearing somewhat perturbed now. "He was supposed to accompany us home."

"He left even before we did," Eliza said, rolling her eyes. "I believe his night was not yet over."

Her mother harrumphed, which said far more than her words ever could. Eliza knew her mother didn't approve of Baxter's life after dark, but he was far too old for her to tell him what to do – not that she ever had before, which might be part of the problem.

Suddenly a bump surprised them as they both jumped, jostled in their seats. They stared at one another for a moment before Eliza's curiosity overtook her and she craned her head out the window while her mother called out to her.

"Eliza! Come back in!"

"There is someone out there," she responded as the driver glanced over his shoulder.

"Apologies, my lady, I tried to stop the horses too abruptly when I saw people in the road ahead. We're slowing now."

Eliza peered into the darkness, trying to make out who it was and what she was seeing. The streets were otherwise deserted, but she could have sworn that was Fitz in front of them – unless he had become so ingrained in her thoughts that she was seeing him everywhere.

He stood to the side closest to the buildings behind him, and another, much larger man was next to him, holding something out toward him.

Just then light glinted off the object between them, and Eliza gasped as she realized what it was – a pistol. Pointed at Fitz. It was him. She was sure of it.

"Keep going!" she called to the driver.

"But—"

"He's going to kill Fitz!" she exclaimed. "Keep going."

The driver didn't question her, knowing exactly who Fitz was and his ties to the family. He snapped the reins, urged the horses on, and, despite the object in their path, they continued forward.

The man looked up at the last moment, his gun discharging as he tried to jump out of the way, missing the horses but not the wheel of the carriage.

Eliza looked back as the carriage continued forward, only to see both men lying on the ground.

And with them, Eliza's heart.

CHAPTER 4

Fitz blinked rapidly as the night sky high above him came back into focus.

For a moment there, he thought he had left this earth, waking to whatever world next awaited him, but then the pebbles of the road beneath him bit into his back, telling him that his time had not yet come.

He ran his hands over himself, feeling for blood or bullet holes, but they came away dry. Thank goodness.

"Fitz!"

He pushed himself up on his elbows, starting when he noticed the big man lying on the ground next to him. Ignoring the call for a moment, he snaked his arm beneath the man, grunting as his hand wrapped around the pistol. He carefully pulled it out, wary that the big man might wake up and finish the job.

The large gash on the side of his attacker's head, however, might mean he was safe.

With the wood of the still-warm pistol in his hand, Fitz finally allowed himself to look up as a flurry of skirts and concern came crashing toward him.

"Eliza?" he said with confusion as she gripped his shoulders tightly while leaning back and running her eyes over him.

"Are you alive? Shot? Injured?" she fired toward him.

He couldn't help the slight laugh that emerged in response to her onslaught of questions.

"I am well. At least, as far as I can tell."

It was only then he noticed the red smear of blood on her cheek, and he reached up, brow furrowed, to wipe it away.

As he did, he realized that it was not her blood that marked her but rather his own, and it was dripping down his arm.

"You are hurt!" she said, with more accusation in her tone than concern.

"Just a scrape," he said, waving it away. "I'm fine. Better than this knave here," he said, waving his hand to the man beside him.

"Was he robbing you?" she asked, standing now as her mother approached.

"I suppose," Fitz said, not wanting to share the truth.

"Lord Fitzroy!" Lady Willoughby exclaimed, her expression matching her daughter's as she rushed forward, although she stopped short of touching him as Eliza had. "Are you well?"

"We were just assessing that," he said as he gingerly pushed himself off of the ground and up to stand before them. "I believe I shall be fine."

He looked at the man on the ground once more, sorely wanting to determine if he was still alive and, if so, to question him as to who he was and what he was doing here.

If he did so, however, he would have to explain himself to the women in front of him, and he had no interest in telling them about this apparent plot to do away with him – nor how he had discovered it.

He had thought that Madeline might have been putting him on, but this was no prank.

Suddenly, the past few minutes came rushing back, as Fitz recalled the resolve that crossed the man's face moments before he pulled the trigger. Then, how he had rushed toward him at the very moment the gun went off, and then how his attacker had suddenly and unexpectedly come flying forward into him, all of it seeming to happen at once. He had been so focused on his impending death that he hadn't realized in conscious thought that there had been a carriage headed toward them. Which meant--

"Did you... run him over?"

Mother and daughter exchanged a look before beginning their story together.

"I'm not sure if 'run him over' is the expression I would use," Eliza said matter-of-factly.

"Perhaps he was unfortunate enough to have been clipped by our carriage wheel," her mother said, a look of contrived innocence crossing her face. "I am very glad that you are well, Lord Fitzroy."

"Yes, of course," he murmured, trying not to laugh at the two women before him who could likely pose more of a threat to the criminal underworld than any Bow Street Runner ever could, were they to put their minds to it. "Well, I shall be on my way, then. We wouldn't want him to come back to consciousness and find two beautiful women standing before him."

"Oh, Lord Fitzroy, you are too kind," Lady Willoughby said with a large smile, while Eliza rolled her eyes. "We must see you home after this ordeal you have been through. Come into the carriage. You do not live far from us."

"Thank you, but I shall be fine walking."

"I would not hear of it," Lady Willoughby said, placing her hands on her hips. "How could I look your mother in the eye if I left you here after such a traumatic incident? Come. Now."

It seemed he had no choice. He chuckled as he followed

the women up into the carriage. Before he ascended the steps, he stopped and laid a hand quickly on their driver's shoulder. "Thank you," he said in a low voice. "Truly."

The man nodded in response before Fitz joined the ladies within, taking a seat next to Eliza facing forward while her mother perched on the opposing seat.

"Where were you walking home from?" Eliza was not one to mince words.

"A club," he answered honestly.

"Was Baxter there?" her mother asked, fortunately cutting off Eliza.

"Ahh, there are many clubs throughout London," he said, not wanting to answer in the affirmative. "Baxter—" he stopped, realizing suddenly that he was speaking to the man's mother and sister, "—enjoys visiting a wide variety of them."

Eliza snorted at that, obviously knowing exactly what he meant, while her mother pressed her lips together.

"You smell like perfume," Eliza said, wrinkling her nose.

She shifted away from him slightly, and he immediately missed her presence. Why did he feel the need to explain that the perfume was no cause for concern?

"I spent a great deal of the evening dancing," he said, clearing his throat. "It must be from one of the ladies."

"It smells cheap."

"Are you suddenly a perfumer?"

"No, but I am a woman who wears perfume."

That he knew. Hers smelled like jasmine – sweet, exotic, and adventurous. Just like her.

"We should not judge, Eliza," her mother said softly, and Fitz was suddenly extremely grateful that she was here, even if it meant that she had seen him at such a low moment.

"Nothing to concern yourself with, ladies. I was simply gambling."

"You do not like to gamble," Eliza said, and he turned to her in astonishment.

"Why would you think that?" he asked, mostly surprised that she would know so much about him and wondering why she had paid such close attention.

"Baxter loves to play cards and you always refuse to join in," she said. It was too dark to see her expression, but her tone was challenging him to prove her wrong. "You only gamble if you are betting on yourself in a competition of skill."

He opened his mouth to respond, before shutting it firmly once more. She was right. And yet he didn't think it was something anyone else had ever noticed.

"Well," Lady Willoughby said as they pulled up in front of Fitz's townhouse. "No more taking late-night gambles walking alone, do you hear me, Lord Fitzroy?"

"Agreed, Lady Willoughby," he said. "Thank you for the escort. And thank you again for your assistance."

"Assistance?" Eliza repeated, those blue-green eyes of hers wide in the light that emerged from the open door of his townhouse. He didn't need to turn around to know that at least one of his sisters stood in the doorway, likely wondering just whose carriage had conveyed him home at this time of night. "We saved your life!"

"Very well," he said with a sigh. "Thank you for saving my life."

He turned, finding four pairs of eyes upon him, and he left the two women behind to face the eight that awaited him within.

It had already been a long night, and he had a feeling that it wasn't over yet.

* * *

ELIZA PACED the drawing room the next morning.

The sun was shining through the front window, the floral arrangements her mother ensured were well tended backdropping the landscape beyond, and she had every reason to welcome the day ahead.

Yet she couldn't shake the feeling that there was more to Fitz's story from last night.

She shouldn't care. She should leave it be and allow him to deal with it.

And yet, she was friends with his sisters. She owed it to them to make sure all was well.

At least, that was what she told herself.

"Mother!" she called up the staircase, wishing her mother would descend earlier in the mornings. Eliza spent far too much time waiting for her.

"Yes?" came her mother's voice, trilling from upstairs.

"Do you have plans for today?"

"Not at the moment."

"We should visit Lady Fitzroy."

Her mother appeared at the top of the stairs, a vision in dark pink, her hair still as dark and curly as Eliza's own. Eliza was fortunate to share so many of her mother's traits.

"Lady Fitzroy?" her mother repeated, raising her brows.

"I would like to ensure all is well after last night. And I had such good conversations with Henrietta and Sloane at the dance. I wouldn't mind seeing them again."

Her mother slowly descended the staircase, finally stopping at the bottom landing. "This has nothing to do with Lord Fitzroy?"

"No," Eliza said, trying to appear affronted. "Why would it?"

Her mother eyed her knowingly as she swept past her. "You were very concerned when he appeared injured last night."

"He is a family friend!" Eliza protested.

"Yes, that he is," her mother said, walking into the breakfast room, even though it was now past noon. Eliza followed her, taking a seat as she watched her mother fill her plate from the sideboard. "However, a family friend can make as good of a match – if not better – than most gentlemen. We know him, we know his family, and he is a good man."

Eliza gaped at her mother. "Is he truly, though?"

"He is a flirt, yes," her mother said, looking her way with her lips curled into a smile. "But that doesn't mean he would make a bad husband."

Eliza snorted as she sat down across from her mother.

"It might," she retorted. "I don't want a man who flirts with every woman he encounters. I want a man like Father, who is utterly devoted to his wife."

"That I am," her father said, choosing that moment to join them. He placed a kiss first on the top of Eliza's head and then on his wife's cheek before he took a seat himself. Eliza knew he had been up for hours, and this was already his second meal of the day, but he enjoyed spending time with them so always made a point to join his wife once she arose. "Where is Baxter?" he said, looking around.

"Here I am!" Baxter said, casually strolling into the room. Eliza wrinkled her nose as she smelled smoke, alcohol, and cheap perfume that reminded her of that which had been cloying to Fitz.

"Have you just returned home now?" she asked, aghast.

"No," he said defensively, obviously lying.

"Where were you?" she asked, and he eyed her before looking around the table at the three of them.

"Are you sure you want to know?"

"I suppose not," Eliza said, crossing her arms over her chest. "Have you spoken to Lord Fitzroy?"

"To Fitz? Not since last night. Why?" He looked up from the toast he was eating, likely to try to relieve any ill effects from the night before, suddenly realizing that there might be an issue of concern.

"Oh dear," their mother said, abandoning her obvious disapproval of her son. "You will never believe what happened."

She proceeded to tell Baxter of the events of the previous night, playing up their coming to Fitz's rescue, even though Eliza remembered it differently. She certainly couldn't recall her mother being the one to urge the driver on.

"Goodness," Baxter murmured as he lifted a scone to his mouth now. "And I thought I was only hearing rumors."

"So, you did know about it?" Eliza attempted to clarify, but he shook his head.

"Not about a man trying to kill Fitz. I heard another rumor. Of someone trying to poison him."

"Poison!" Eliza exclaimed. "Who?"

"Doesn't matter," Baxter said, shaking his head. "What does matter is that someone is obviously out to get him."

"Why?" Eliza said, her stomach beginning to churn. "Is someone trying to claim the title?"

"Doubtful," Baxter said. "I'm not even sure who would inherit."

"If I had to guess," their father chimed in, which caused them all to turn his way, for his contributions to conversations were so rare that they were always worth listening to, "it has something to do with what he is proposing to bring to the House of Lords."

"Which is?" his wife asked expectantly.

"I really shouldn't say."

"Oh, for goodness' sake, Clifford, if you mention it, you must finish the story."

Eliza had to hide her smile behind her hand, for she knew that her father wasn't winning this one. He should have known better before he raised the subject.

"Very well. He has been meeting with a social reformer and political activist, as well as a member of parliament, about repealing the Combination Acts."

"Pardon me?" said Baxter, who had no prior knowledge of his friend's views judging from the expression on his face.

"He is trying to rally some of the other lords to provide their support as well. The trade unions feel they have been suppressed by the laws, and Fitz agrees that this has only led to clandestine activity."

"Why does he care?" Baxter asked with a snort, earning himself the ire of his mother and sister. Sometimes Eliza wondered if she and her brother had truly been raised by the same parents.

"I suppose he has always preferred that things come to light," Eliza couldn't help but note.

"He wouldn't be killed for it, in any case. It's not as though he is irreplaceable on this," Baxter said, sitting back in his chair.

"Well," Eliza's mother said, placing her fork down and clasping her hands together as she looked around at the rest of them. "There is only one thing to do about it."

They all waited expectantly, knowing she would finish her idea shortly.

"We visit his townhouse and find out."

CHAPTER 5

Fitz awoke that morning with aches in muscles he hadn't even known existed. He felt like a man twice his age as he walked down the stairs, only to be met by the entirety of his family, all with many questions and no offer of reprieve.

"Are you going to tell us what happened, Fitz, or not?" asked Georgina with a frown as she crossed her arms over her chest. They had all gathered in the drawing room, awaiting him until he finally descended. He had taken his time, both because his entire body was in pain and also because he had hoped that if he waited long enough, they all would have gone off in their own pursuits.

He had been wrong.

"Nothing happened. There was an incident on my way home," he explained as patiently as he could. "A man tried to rob me and then there was a carriage accident. I came away unscathed but for a few bruises. I lost nothing and every part is intact."

Except, perhaps, his honor.

"I sense there is more to this," Dot said, but before she could continue, a knock sounded on the door.

"Yes?" Fitz's mother called out and the butler stepped into the room.

"Lady Willoughby and Lady Eliza have come to call."

"Oh," his mother said, her lips pursing together as she tried to decide what to do. "As it happens, we are in the middle of something."

"Best show them in," Fitz said with a sigh. "They are part of this and will likely have the same questions."

He could also keep his story straight if he only had to tell it once.

"What do they have to do with it?" Henrietta asked, and he had just enough time to explain their presence in the carriage – for he knew Eliza would tell his sisters anyway – when the women in question walked in.

"Oh, Lady Willoughby, thank you so much," his mother said, walking toward her friend and wrapping her in a very rare embrace. "You saved my son."

Lady Willoughby fanned her reddening cheeks. "Oh, I wouldn't say that," she said, although she clearly meant otherwise. "Our timing was fortunate, is all."

Fitz's mother led the new arrivals to the corner of the sofa where Fitz had previously been sitting, leaving him to stand in front of the lot of them as though he was on stage, there to entertain them.

Not that he would have been able to sit still while telling this story. He tried to stand in one position, rocking from his heels to his toes and back again as he cleared his throat, but soon enough he found himself bouncing and he found the best way to contain all of the energy that was trying to convince him to run out of here and away from all of these questioning eyes was to pace back and forth.

"So, as you were saying, a thief accosted you in the middle of the street – just outside of Hanover Square – with no one else about, and then Lady Willoughby and Lady Eliza happened to come along, knock over the man, and save your life?" Sloane asked, setting her chin on her fist, her elbow resting on the arm of the sofa.

Fitz began to chew nervously on his thumbnail.

"Yes, I suppose that's the way of it."

"But that's not all," Eliza said nearly triumphantly, and a chill ran down Fitz's spine. Did she know the rest of it? No. She couldn't. There was no possible way that her life could intersect with Madeline's, and even if it had, how could the activities of last night ever have returned to her?

"Lady Eliza," he said through gritted teeth, fixing an expression toward her that he hoped was telling her not to speak another word, and yet every pair of eyes in the room likely saw his face and knew there was more to this story. "I do not believe there is any more to share."

"No?" she said, lifting a brow, openly defying him. "You were not nearly poisoned?"

"Poisoned!" Fitz couldn't be sure who said it. It seemed to be a melody of his mother and sisters all voicing their concerns together.

He sighed, resigned to his fate.

"When I was out last night, I was offered a drink. Someone was paid to try to poison me," he said, finally accepting that he had no choice but to tell the truth, for it seemed that it was bound and determined to come out, no matter what he did. "How did you know of this, Lady Eliza?"

"Baxter," she said, even as her mother tried to shush her.

Eliza turned to her. "If we are all truth-telling, then I must join in, must I not?"

Her mother seemed resigned to that logic, as she nodded slowly. Damn Munroe.

"Did you drink any of it?" Dot asked, already standing and walking toward him, but he swatted his sister's hands away.

"No!" he exclaimed. "I'm fine. Healthy as ever. Didn't have a drop."

"You're healthy for now," said Georgina, always looking for the worst possible outcome of every situation. "But that could certainly change as whoever has ill designs on you seems determined to continue."

"She's right, unfortunately," said Dot, glancing over with concern at their youngest sisters, Betsy and Daphne. "What are you going to do?"

"Do?" Fitz repeated. "Why, I am going to try to get to the bottom of this, to determine just who would want me disposed of and why they have gone to such lengths in attempting to do so."

"How do you propose to do this detective work?" Dot asked, crossing her arms over her chest, staring him down.

"Do you have no faith in me, Dot?"

"What are you going to do, *charm* your murderer?"

"Attempted murderer."

She rolled her eyes at him, and he sighed, rubbing a hand over his face.

"Speaking of detectives," Eliza chimed in, "why do you not hire one?"

"A detective?"

"Yes," she said slowly, as though she was talking to a child. "Someone who has the expertise to do this work."

He should have thought of that. Not that he was going to admit as such.

"Maybe I will."

"Best do it soon, before this *attempted* murderer succeeds."

"In the meantime," Henrietta said, "we should probably go to the country, should we not?"

"We should," said Sloane and his mother at the same time he answered, "Absolutely not."

"How could we not?" Sloane said, her mouth agape. "Fitz, this is serious. You are not invincible."

"I've escaped two attempts, have I not?"

"But you might not be so lucky next time," his mother

said, her voice low and her expression grave. "What would we do without you, Fitz?"

That stopped him. He hadn't given much thought to what would become of all of his sisters – and his mother – if this plot against him was successful. He had only considered how much he had to do before his time here was done.

"I suppose we could only hope the next heir is more responsible," he said, attempting a joke, but it fell flat. He lifted his hands in supplication. "I have important work to do. We are still in the season. Parliament is in session. I—"

"There's something else you are not considering."

All eyes turned toward Eliza – including his own. Why did she have to look so stunning sitting there, wearing nothing but a plain morning dress? It was as though the less finery she wore, the more her natural beauty shone through. Annoying.

"What is it, Eliza?" he asked before his mother turned her head to him sharply. "Lady Eliza," he amended.

"If you stay in London, it is not just *you* who could be in danger. Your entire family could be at risk."

He opened his mouth to offer a retort but the only thing that emerged was a sigh. For as much as he hated to admit it, she was right. And there was nothing he could do about it.

Except pack up his family and journey to Essex.

* * *

ELIZA FOLLOWED Sloane and Henrietta out of the drawing room after Fitz told them both it was time to pack. Just as they reached the landing, a knock sounded on the door, and Eliza hung back, peeking over the railing, out of sight, to see who had come to call.

"Lord Mandrake for Lord Fitzroy," came a dull voice that she recognized. "Or Lady Dot, if she is home."

"One moment, my lord," the butler said before leaving the

man at the front door. He returned moments later, his steps quick and efficient. "My apologies, my lord, but neither Lord Fitzroy nor Lady Dot are currently available to accept callers."

There was a loud sniff that Eliza assumed was Lord Mandrake showing his displeasure.

"Tomorrow, then."

"Perhaps," the butler returned, "although Lord Fitzroy and his family may be leaving London for a time. May I pass on a message?"

There was a clicking of Lord Mandrake's tongue against his teeth before he responded, "Tell him that I must talk to him. I have intentions toward Lady Dot, and I mean to act upon them. Tell him that if he would like to marry off his sisters, I have a perfectly good offer for the first. Tell him he should put aside his dislike for me and do right by his family."

"Ah—very good, my lord. I will do so," the butler said before ushering the man out. Lord Mandrake had no idea who he was dealing with. Dot was not one to bow to a man who ordered her about, nor was Fitz the type of man who would ever let someone he disdained become close to his family.

"Eliza! Where are you?"

She put aside her musings to hurry after Henrietta, who was waiting at the end of the corridor, hands on her hips. They entered the large room the twin sisters shared, Eliza taking a seat on the edge of the bed as a maid bustled about the room, helping her ladies. Henrietta was actively participating in the preparations while Sloane was draped across one of the beds.

"As much as I love our country home, I will miss you dreadfully," Henrietta said, going through her wardrobe.

Even though she knew her argument had caused Fitz to agree to take his family to the country, Eliza hated that they were going. Henrietta and Sloane were two of her closest friends besides Siena, who she now saw so infrequently, as she lived just outside the city.

Eliza glanced over at the other bed, finding that Sloane did not seem overly concerned with their upcoming departure, her arms and legs spread wide like a star, her eyes closed.

"Sloane?" she asked. "Are you all right?"

"Fine," Sloane said from her prostrate position. "Just packing."

"You are not moving."

"I first visualize in my mind what I might need. Then it takes far less time to pack it all together."

"That is called laziness," Henrietta remarked, causing Eliza to laugh. She always wondered how two sisters could look so alike and be born at the same time yet be so incredibly different from one another.

"Respect my process, Hen."

Eliza considered how much fun the three of them – four, when Siena had joined them – had always had together, and wondered when she would next see them.

"Do you think you will be bored out in the country?" she asked, addressing her question to Henrietta since Sloane seemed otherwise occupied.

Henrietta shrugged. "I'm not entirely sure. I most often enjoy it, but then we are usually spending quite a bit of time at balls and parties and the like. With most people in London for the Season, I can imagine it will be much duller. That being said, we are fortunate that we have so many of us to entertain one another."

A snore came from Sloane's bed and a pained expression crossed Henrietta's face. "Perhaps I will be bored, after all."

Eliza couldn't help but laugh at that, and as dire as the situation facing Fitz's life was, she embraced her friends and wished them the best of luck in solving this situation quickly so that they might return to London.

At this rate, she would have no acquaintances left in the city.

Perhaps she should go stay with Siena for a time, she mused an hour later as she followed her mother into the carriage.

But no, Siena and her new husband were far too wrapped up in one another. She would not want to disturb their newfound happiness. Not yet.

Then there was her plan. She had set a goal for herself at the beginning of this Season. One that she had kept secret from everyone, even Siena. If anyone were to discover just what she was intent on accomplishing, she would become the greatest scandal of the Season without even taking action.

She had stumbled across a book Baxter had snuck into the house. Where he had happened upon it, she had no idea, but she had been intrigued as to why suddenly her brother, who barely ever picked up a book, seemed so captivated by this one.

When she stole it one day, she was shocked to discover its contents and became fascinated with experiencing the pleasure that could exist between a man and a woman. After she overcame her surprise, however, she became interested.

Needless to say, Baxter had never recovered his book.

Eliza had remained curious. And her curiosity was yet to be answered.

Although she supposed it could wait. She had gone this long without any discoveries. What was a little more time?

"What's on your mind?" her mother asked, and Eliza choked at the thought of actually sharing it with her mother, covering her surprise with a faked cough.

"Just that I will now have more friends leaving London in the middle of the Season."

"You make friends everywhere you go," her mother said, waving her hand in the air.

"Yes, but I like *my* friends," Eliza said. "How long do you think they will be away?"

"I suppose until they determine who is out to take the life of Lord Fitzroy," her mother said with a shiver, and Eliza felt her pang of uneasiness at the thought of someone after him. She had thought it was because she was concerned as to what it could mean for his sisters.

But what if there was more? He was an attractive man to be sure. Even if he was an utter boar sometimes.

Perhaps she could find answers to all of her problems at the same time, she mused. It just might take some convincing.

But convincing she could do.

CHAPTER 6

Fitz was bored.

He usually didn't mind spending time at his estate. It provided him a respite, a break where he could recover and simply be himself.

But then, he was never usually here while Parliament was in session, and he was missing some of the most important discussions in the country.

Discussions that were so far from those he was currently involved in, which, at the moment, were centered around whether one of the maids and the stablehand were involved in a torrid love affair.

"I am bored," his mother declared, echoing his own thoughts, once the conversation had concluded. She threw her book down in front of her, causing the rest of them to look up at her in surprise.

"Bored?" Sloane repeated. "Why?"

"There is nowhere to go, nothing to do, no one to see," she said with a sigh. "Everyone we normally spend time with is in London."

"We could go to the village," Henrietta suggested, but their mother clucked her tongue.

"We cannot. Then everyone will know we are here."

"I'm sure they already do," Georgina said. "Servants talk."

"True, but to be out in the open would be much more dangerous," Henrietta argued, to which Dot nodded her head in agreement.

All of Fitz's sisters had accepted their country stay, except Dot. While she had eventually agreed, that didn't mean that she was particularly pleased about leaving the women she had committed to. Fitz had suggested those women could perhaps find a midwife they might have to actually pay to which Dot told him he was missing the point of everything, and he had raised his hands in defeat and given up the argument.

"Perhaps one of my friends will come to stay with us," his mother said, causing Fitz to raise his eyebrows.

"And just who will you invite?" he asked.

"Does it matter?"

He laughed at her question. "Of course it does! I am in residence with nowhere else to go."

"Very well," she said with a stern expression. "I sent off a few letters, but I assume that no one is going to respond. Who would want to come to a country home in the middle of the Season when there is so much happening in London and most friends have daughters to marry off?"

Immediately his stomach began to turn as he wondered if Lady Willoughby would have received one such letter. He wasn't certain he could handle more time with her daughter, Eliza, especially if they were going to be in such proximity.

"I'm not certain—"

"Oh, yes, please do, Mother!" Henrietta said. "We would have such fun."

"Perhaps I shall invite a *few* of my friends," his mother continued. "Or there is always Lady Nottingham and her daughters…"

His mother looked slightly queasy for a moment and with

good reason. Lady Nottingham was an absolute bore, and his mother usually avoided her. She must be desperate if she was considering her company. The girls, however, enjoyed Lady Nottingham's daughters, and they visited now and again.

"I would rather you did not let the entirety of the *ton* know where we are and why we are here," Fitz said through gritted teeth.

"Of course not," his mother said, turning her head toward him sharply. "Do you think me stupid?"

"Never."

"I have told none of them that you are here, pretending that you are in London."

"And if they do decide to visit? Am I going to hide the entire time?"

"No," his mother said with a snort. "We will then say you just arrived."

"Is it so terrible to be spending time amongst family at this beautiful estate?" Fitz asked, even though he was nearly dying of boredom himself.

"Yes, Fitz. It is," Sarah said before sneezing dramatically, as she always did when they were in the country, although Fitz had no idea why.

"Well," he said, standing and clapping his hands against his legs. "I am going for a ride. I shall see you all at dinner time."

He left, rubbing his hand against his temple, hoping that the private detective he had hired would complete the job soon.

For he wasn't sure how much longer he could stand this.

* * *

ELIZA BOUNCED her foot over her knee, her legs crossed as she sat back against the squab of the carriage.

"I should be telling you that your posture should be much

improved," her mother murmured as she stared out the window, although she did not seem particularly inclined to enforce her words.

"I will improve it if I am in company with anyone else," Eliza said. "You know that I behave myself when required."

"True," her mother said, inclining her head, and Eliza gave in to her impulse to lean over and kiss her mother on the cheek.

"What was that for?" her mother asked, her eyes widening slightly.

"For being you," Eliza said with a smile of affection. "I am well aware of how fortunate I am to have you."

"That is very kind, Eliza," her mother said, leaning forward and patting her leg. "Thank you."

As Appleton Manor came into view, Eliza's heart started to beat quickly and, she thought, somewhat erratically.

"Did you tell Lady Fitzroy that we would be coming?" she asked, wondering what Fitz was thinking about their arrival. Not that it mattered. They were nothing to one another.

"I did write to her, but I'm not sure if we will have arrived before the letter," her mother said. "She seemed so concerned that I thought it best we come nearly immediately."

Eliza nodded absentmindedly. This is what she had wanted – to see her friends again much sooner rather than later, and Appleton was a beautiful place.

It didn't take much intelligence to know what the problem was.

Fitz. The lord of the manor himself.

She contained her sigh as the carriage started up the long drive, and Eliza wondered how much she would be seeing of him. She supposed she would soon find out.

By the time the carriage pulled up, the butler and housekeeper were already standing out front, and once Eliza and her mother started up the steps, Lady Fitzroy had joined them.

"Lady Willoughby!" she exclaimed, holding her hands out, taking Eliza's mother's in a firm clasp before they kissed one another's faces. "What are you doing here?"

"You wrote to me!" Eliza's mother exclaimed with a laugh. "You said you must see me immediately."

"I did?"

"You did."

She glanced at Fitz, who lifted his brows as though to say he saw right through his mother's pretense, although there was a smile on his face as Eliza was aware that despite any bluster he might have, he had a soft spot for his mother and sisters.

"Baxter didn't join?" he asked, stepping forward, welcoming the two of them.

"Baxter?" Eliza said with a snort. "Of course not. We are not nearly close enough to any bar—"

"Eliza!" her mother intervened, and Eliza snapped her mouth shut, realizing she was turning herself into a liar as she had just finished telling her mother she knew how to behave.

"Baxter is otherwise occupied," she substituted with a demure smile that had her mother rolling her eyes, but she didn't miss Fitz's smirk, which he quickly wiped off of his face before her mother noticed.

"Lady Fitzroy, it is lovely to see you," Eliza said, changing the subject. "I have so missed all of your daughters."

"Oh dear, I do wish I had received your letter first," Lady Fitzroy said with a pained expression on her face. "They have just left, but for Betsy and Daphne."

"Left?" Eliza repeated, her face falling, trying to curb her disappointment as they hadn't known she was coming, so it wasn't their fault. "To where have they gone?"

"To Lady Nottingham's estate. It is only a few hours' ride. They were becoming so bored here that they asked to spend some time there with her daughters, and I…" she waved her hands in the air, "decided that I could not join them at this time."

Eliza completely understood. She knew Lady Nottingham and couldn't imagine spending much time in her presence, especially without anyone else for company. One of her daughters had married beneath her station – there was something of a scandal there if she remembered correctly – and her family lived at the estate.

"Well, hopefully, they will return soon," she said instead, trying to hide her disappointment. Betsy and Daphne were wonderful young women, but they were just that – young. At least ten years her junior, if she remembered correctly.

And then there was Fitz. She stole a glance at him as he stood, rocking back and forth on his heels as he always did. Did he care that she and her mother had arrived so suddenly and without prior warning? She knew they could be somewhat impulsive, but she had thought they would be welcomed warmly. What did he think of them now spending time at Appleton without the presence of his sisters, which had always prevented Fitz from speaking to her alone?

Eliza had accompanied her mother because she was bored without her friends. Now it appeared that she was going to continue to be bored without them, only she no longer had the distractions of London. She was going to have to come up with distractions of another kind.

She glanced over at Fitz as an idea took shape in her mind. One that was probably ill-advised, yet... perhaps she could defeat her boredom while accomplishing her goals simultaneously.

Eliza was aware that she would soon have to marry and settle down. She just wanted to have a little fun first.

And if there was one thing that could be said about Fitz, it was that he was fun.

Just how much fun, she was about to find out.

* * *

"Stay away from Lady Eliza."

It was a mantra that Fitz had continued to murmur to himself over and over since she and her mother had appeared at Appleton yesterday.

He had his plan. Have some fun, and then settle down with a demure young lady who would take care of his mother and his sisters, marry them off and bring him all of the respectability that he wasn't able to acquire himself.

Eliza didn't fit into that plan.

He couldn't have fun with her – she was an innocent young lady of the nobility, and his sisters' friend at that. He couldn't marry her either – she was the exact opposite of what he needed.

She was loud, exuberant, adventurous – far too much like himself.

And yet, he couldn't help but be drawn to her.

He had all but avoided her at Greystone. He could do the same here as well.

Only, now, something had shifted. He had become aware of her, and he couldn't be entirely certain of why. Perhaps it was because he had begun to consider marrying and knew that his time to appreciate a woman such as her was coming to an end. Perhaps it was from their dance. He had felt her body against his, and he had liked it far more than he would have preferred.

Or perhaps it was because, as much as he didn't want to admit it, even to himself, he had spent enough time with her now to know that he appreciated her sense of humor, her wit, her charm, the way she looked at life.

Her beauty didn't help matters.

With all of this on his mind, he did the only thing he could think of to cool off his ardor. Taking a circuitous route through the house so that he could emerge outside through the terrace doors, he left the women to their needlepoint or tea or whatever it was they occupied themselves with and he marched through the gardens surrounding the house to seek out the one place that he could find both solace and respite.

The lake.

It was nestled away from the house, close enough that the water was in view from the windows of the upper story, but not so close that anyone might be able to see exactly what he was doing. There were enough trees surrounding the lake that he knew which parts of it provided enough coverage that he would be hidden from view – which was exactly what he needed at the moment.

He slipped through the trees, pushing away the branches that threatened to reach out and smack him in the face, somehow knowing he was being an idiot. But no mind.

Around the edges of the lake, wildflowers bloomed in vibrant colors, creating a picturesque scene. A gentle breeze rustled the tall reeds along the shore, the soothing sound calming his heart that was beating faster than it should have been, lush green trees that surrounded the lake reflecting off the surface of the calm water. The sky was somewhat grey today, and yet the colors of this respite in the middle of the chaos of his life were enough to bring him peace.

He didn't hesitate as he stripped off his jacket, his carefully tied cravat, his waistcoat and his shirt, shucking his breeches without worry that anyone would see him unclothed. And if they did, well, he was proud of his appearance. Unless it was a member of his family happening upon him, they could take his fill.

Knowing where the deep parts of the lake began, Fitz perfectly executed a dive, then propelled himself forward, allowing the cool water to wash over him until he broke through the surface, coming up for air when he could hold his breath no longer.

He blinked, clearing the water from his eyes, whipping his head back and forth to clear his hair from his face.

Suddenly he stopped, sensing that he was no longer alone. He whipped his head from one side to the other until the figure came into view.

There, on the far bank, stood a woman. Lilac dress. Dark hair. A grin that he couldn't see but just knew covered her face.

Eliza.

CHAPTER 7

*E*liza had wondered if this was a bad idea.

But then she had seen Fitz standing there on the shore with nothing between him and the sun above them.

And had a feeling that this was one of the best ideas she had ever had.

She hadn't meant to spy upon him without revealing herself. She had seen him leave the house despite his obvious attempts to do so surreptitiously. She had followed him, considering that now might be the only time she would be able to have this conversation with him.

Then, before she could catch up and announce herself, he had begun to strip, and she had stood there behind a tree, unable to move for fear that in doing so she would announce herself, and she had a feeling that he wouldn't be pleased she had followed him here when he preferred solitude.

For he wouldn't be able to swim naked alone in her presence.

At least, not yet.

She smiled wickedly as she took a seat on a large rock on the embankment. She could see what had drawn him to this area of the estate. It truly was beautiful here, the waters reflecting the grey of the sky, melding with the green of the surrounding trees. She tapped her foot impatiently, wondering if now was the time to have this conversation, or if she should leave before he noticed her.

It took her too long to decide, however, for suddenly he broke through the surface, startling her, and she clenched her hands tightly together when he cast his eyes upon her.

"What are you doing here?" he called out, and she couldn't tell whether or not there was anger in his tone. More shocked resignation, she decided.

"I came to speak to you," she said, telling herself that she was not the type of woman to shirk from a man's response. Especially a man who was never angry. This was Fitz. She was sure he would be happy once he learned just why she had come.

"Could you not have spoken to me at any moment in the house? When I was clothed?" he asked as he trod water. The lake must be rather deep there.

"I could have, but this is not a conversation that I wanted anyone to overhear."

"That is a frightening prospect."

"Would you like to come closer? I'd prefer not to shout," she said, already slightly embarrassed at what she was about to ask. She didn't need the entire estate to overhear her.

"Very well," he grumped, swimming toward her until he stopped about half the distance closer, enough that she could speak in quieter tones, and he could stand on what appeared to be the lake's bottom beneath him, but not so close that she could see what was hiding beneath the surface.

A pity.

"What can I do for you, Lady Eliza?" he asked as though he was at a society event. It made her laugh.

"Are you bored, Fitz?" she asked, suddenly unable to get right to the point. It seemed far too forward, even for her.

"Bored? Now? Eliza, I am swimming in the lake on my

family's estate in the middle of a Season in which I am supposed to be finding a wife and introducing changes to the law that have never been heard of before. Yesterday I engaged in a conversation about which servant the scullery maid prefers. So yes, I am bored."

He lifted his hands and threw them down into the water, causing splashes to reach the hem of her dress.

"Sorry," he murmured. "And in case you were wondering, *I* think she fancies the stablehand."

"It's fine," she said, trying to keep her chipper tone intact. "As it happens, I agree with you on that. Now, I also thought that my time here would be different. You can understand that I assumed Henrietta and Sloane would be here, as well as the rest of your sisters."

"Of course," he said, obviously curious about where she was going with this.

"Well, I have a proposition for you. One which would solve the boredom we are each dealing with."

He waited, one eyebrow lifted.

She took a breath, the words rushing forward.

"You see, for some time now, I have been very interested in the pleasures that can be found between man and woman."

His jaw dropped so suddenly she wondered whether he was going to faint. She could swim, but she wasn't sure she could swim well enough to rescue him from the bottom of the lake.

"I know that I will need to marry soon, and I understand that the relations between husband and wife can be... perfunctory."

"I-I suppose that depends on who you marry," he said, finally finding his voice, although his eyes remained round.

"Yes, I suppose, but the problem is, one would not know what type of husband she has until it is too late." She sighed. "Quite annoying."

He nodded slowly, jerkily, and she took that as a sign to continue.

"I decided that, before I marry, I would like to explore the pleasures that could be found so that I don't go the entirety of my life without experiencing them. That being said, I would like to do so safely and with a man whom I can trust. I have been considering options for some time."

He seemed to suddenly understand where she was going with this, as he shook his head and Eliza tried to push down the hurt that he would so quickly dismiss her.

"You are the brother to my friends. Your family is close to mine. You have experience so I would guess that you are proficient in such relations. And I expect you know how to prevent pregnancy, given that I haven't heard talk of you having any bastard children running about. With that being said, I was wondering if, in the time that we are both here at Appleton, you would share some of your expertise?"

He looked so dumbstruck that Eliza stood, prepared to enter the water to attempt to save him from drowning if it came to that.

"Are you going to be all right, Fitz? Perhaps you should come out of the water before you are overcome."

"I am not overcome," he argued. "I am... I am... surprised."

"That is to be understood," she said, knotting her hands together. "If you would like some time to think about this, please take it, although we cannot take overly too much time as soon enough your sisters might return or your detective might do his job and we will have to return to London."

"You have the same prospects as any other young woman. Why this sudden need?"

"I am curious. And I always like to satisfy my curiosity."

"You have listed all of the reasons why me, but... you hate me."

He lifted his eyes to hers, and she was surprised to find some hurt within them.

"I don't *hate* you," she said, telling the truth. "And even if I did, I could hate you on the inside and lie with you on the outside."

He lifted his wet hands, rubbing them over his face.

"All of the reasons you listed for us to be… intimate with one another are also the very reasons we should not be. Your family trusts me. I am trying to be a respected member of Parliament, which isn't easy with my reputation for being something of a scoundrel."

Eliza's heart fell. "So, you are worried that I would cause you greater scandal."

"Yes. No. I don't know."

Eliza nodded, her heart pounding as she asked the next question.

"Could you want me?"

"Am I what?"

"Are you attracted to me?" she asked, knowing that if he said no, it would wreck her, but she needed to know for then she would give up on this entirely. "Are you saying no because you feel that you would be repulsed by me?"

"Absolutely not," he said with such conviction that she believed him and her relief washed over her like a wave. "You are… most attractive."

"Thank goodness," she said, smiling wider than she likely should have.

She looked around her for a moment, knowing that this was her one chance. If she walked away now, it would be easy for him to say no in passing, and then any opportunity she had to reach this goal would be ruined.

She reached behind her, grasping the tie at the bottom of her dress's fastening and releasing it before shrugging her way out of the gown, her arms sliding through first.

"What are you doing?" he asked hoarsely.

"I am coming for a swim."

"No, you are not."

"Yes, I am. I am a fairly good swimmer, and the weather is quite warm."

"Yes, but you—I am—Eliza, this is not a good idea."

From the way he was eyeing her, however, she had a feeling that his words were at odds with his true feelings on the matter. She shed her gown and her stays, leaving just her chemise. She knew that once wet, the thin fabric would provide no barrier whatsoever, but if he said yes to her request, what did it matter?

She slipped off her shoes and stockings, setting her toes in the water, closing her eyes in welcome relief as it washed over them. Heavenly.

She began to wade in and noted that instead of backing away from her, Fitz was taking small steps toward her.

"Are you sure you can swim?" he asked, and she laughed.

"Of course."

He stepped closer, holding out a hand toward her. She took it and allowed him to lead her into the water until they were standing together, an arms-length distance between them. He was breathing heavily, his eyes dark with desire.

"This is a bad idea," he murmured, but inwardly, Eliza had already begun to celebrate, for she could tell that his reservations had begun to fall away from him.

"Don't you love bad ideas?" she asked.

"I do," he admitted. "But I have been trying to leave them behind."

"Sometimes a bad idea can become the best one you have ever had," she countered, taking a small step toward him, noting that he was doing the same, the gap between them closing ever so slowly. "That's where all the fun happens."

"You are no good for me," he murmured, lifting his fingers and running them along the side of her face as she leaned into his touch, shocked at how his caress remained on her face and yet the tremors ran through her entire body, warming her from the inside out to the cool water that surrounded them.

"Say no then," she challenged him, and he groaned as he moved his hands to her hips and hauled her in toward him so that there was no space left between them. His hard, muscular thighs molded against her soft ones, his chest broad and wet, covered in springy hairs beneath her fingertips.

He was so... *masculine,* and despite how difficult it had been to approach him, she was now rather proud of herself for doing so, for this was well worth it.

She was desperate to feel his lips on hers. He would know how to kiss her properly, not like the chaste experiments stolen in corners that she had attempted before.

"Very well," she breathed against his lips, which were but an inch away. "I shall find another to help me in my quest."

That did it – the moment the words were released, he growled, reaching out and wrapping his arms around her back, holding her still as his lips crashed down upon hers.

It was only then that she realized just exactly what she had gotten herself into.

She wasn't sure whether she should be scared or ecstatic.

Either way, this was one adventure that she was glad she hadn't missed, and one thing was for certain – she had chosen the right man.

Of that, she was sure.

CHAPTER 8

Fitz had never been the most rational of men.

That was something he was trying to change.

Eliza, however, had snapped all of the resistance he had been building within himself with her one request.

One request that he didn't have within him to refute.

He had been shocked beyond words when she had approached him with her proposition, but he thought he had managed his response well.

Until she had joined him in the water.

In nothing but her chemise.

He could feel the tips of her pebbled nipples upon his bare chest now, her chemise leaving nothing to the imagination as he kissed her with a fervor he had never known before.

It had to be because she was forbidden, even if he had been the one to have restricted her from himself.

He couldn't consider it any further, however. Not now. For now, his mind had turned off, his desire overtaking it in making all the decisions for his body. Eliza's lips were soft and yielding beneath his, a stark contrast to the heat that blazed between them, cooled only by the water that lapped around their waists. Every touch, every sigh that escaped her sent shivers down his spine, telling him that perhaps she was right. Perhaps a bad idea could become one of the very best.

For in that moment, nothing else mattered except Eliza in his arms. Fitz deepened the kiss, pouring all his longing and passion into it, tasting the sweetness of her surrender.

Her hands roamed over his chest as though she was memorizing every contour of his body with an eagerness that matched his own.

A primal urge awakened within Fitz, a need to possess and protect this woman who had dared to challenge him in ways he never thought possible. Where it had come from, he wasn't sure, but it must have been lying there, dormant, pushed down by his very best of intentions.

They broke apart for air, panting as they stared at one another, and Fitz reached out and wiped away the droplets of water on Eliza's nose that had dripped from his hair onto her face.

"This is madness," he said huskily, unable to help the need that laced his words.

Eliza's laughter rang out like music in the night air. "Madness is just another word for adventure, Fitz," she whispered, her breath warm against his skin, her eyes containing a wildness that mirrored his own.

She was everything he could ever want in a woman and yet the very last woman he needed.

Maybe she was right, however. Maybe they could have some fun without the need for anything more.

He had never been able to help how drawn he was to her and had wondered if kissing her would give him clarity and ease the need for her that had been growing so desperately in his chest.

But instead, it had the exact opposite effect, for now, that desperation had grown nearly to the point that he could no longer contain it.

"I've been trying to avoid adventure," he said with pain. "But it seems it has found me all the same."

"So, what do you think?" she asked, looking up at him through thick lashes. He knew that she had never been one to act with any contrived flirtation, and yet he had never before seen a woman so alluring. But that was just her, in her most purely natural form. "Will you do this? Will you help me?"

His laugh was more of a bark of shock, and before he knew what he was saying, he was lowering his hands.

"After that kiss, Eliza, how could I ever say no?"

The joy that lit her face was worth it all as she wrapped her arms around him and pulled her to him in an embrace, one that he was sure was meant to thank him but had far more effect on him than gratitude.

"Thank you!" she said. "I so appreciate it. You will not regret it."

Those were not the words he wanted to hear, for somehow, they almost seemed like a foreshadowing of their future. Yet the idea of a young woman thanking him for showing her pleasure? It seemed almost too good of a proposal.

Fitz would be a fool to turn down anything that would so favor them both.

So, he decided to pull her close and seal their agreement with a kiss.

* * *

As their lips met again, the world around them seemed to melt away, leaving only the two of them in this bubble where no one else could touch them. The water that surrounded them rippled in reaction to their passion as if trying to mimic the rhythm of their heartbeats.

If Fitz's was beating as hard as hers, then Eliza wondered how they weren't causing tidal waves.

She had always been one to voice her thoughts aloud, and

while Fitz had not denied her, she could admit that it had hurt her some that he would think her such a poor decision.

She was determined to prove him wrong – that she could be with him and enjoy him without giving away her heart.

A thrill of anticipation coursed through Eliza as she moaned softly into the kiss, her hands roaming over Fitz's back, his muscles bunching beneath her touch.

He responded by deepening the kiss, his fingers splaying across her lower back with just the right amount of pressure to hold her steady against him, allowing her to feel his thickness jutting into the bottom of her stomach.

What would it be like to have him inside of her? To have their bodies joined together?

The thought had her pressing even closer against him.

Slowly, Fitz's hands started to move lower, tracing a line over her hip bones, until they stopped an inch above where she ached for him.

"What are you doing?" she asked breathily, gripping his upper arms.

He immediately removed his hands, which was the last thing she wanted from him.

"I'm sorry, I thought you—"

"I was wondering why you stopped!" she said, slapping him lightly on the shoulder, which caused him to jump as he stared at her in surprise.

"Oh," he said. "I thought—"

"I know," she said, taking pity on him. "Which is why I am telling you how I feel. *Don't* stop."

"This is what you truly want?" he said again. "We'll go slow, I promise. I don't want to shock you and before we take this any further, you should know what you are getting into."

"I am well aware," she nearly growled herself, as she was becoming frustrated with all of this talking. She needed more action. "Now, can our lessons begin?"

He nodded slowly, his cheeks reddening at her demands despite the cool water around them.

She stared up at him, hoping he could sense her trust in him, and he nodded, more to himself than to her. He lifted his hands from her hips, reaching toward her in invitation, and she took his palm without hesitation. He led her toward shore, his entire body bare before her, his nakedness almost seeming a point of pride rather than humility.

The shore was grassy, with dark sand leading down to the water. Fitz had come prepared, for he walked over to his pile of clothes and lifted a piece of linen from below it, which he laid out on the soft grass just away from the water, beneath the overhang of branches of the tree above them.

"Lie down," he said gruffly, his eyes running over her body, and Eliza looked down to see that even though she had not waded any further than her waist, her breasts were obvious beneath her chemise as she had been pressed so tightly against Fitz's wet chest. As for her lady parts, well, nothing was hidden from Fitz now.

Eliza was glad when he lay down beside her, for as bold as she was, she was a bit concerned by the size of him. How his manhood was supposed to fit in her, she didn't know, but her book had shown a great variety of ways it could do so.

As they lay down side by side, their bodies still touching, he reached out and traced circles on her palm with his fingers, the sensation making her shiver. She closed her eyes, savoring the feeling of his touch, noting that he certainly knew what he was doing to relax her.

Fitz must have sensed that she was giving into what he was offering, for his fingers traveled, further exploring her.

"Before we start, you best understand what you are asking for," he said, taking her hand and lifting it, causing her entire body to jolt when he placed it on his hard length.

Her eyes flew open, widening in surprise.

"Do you feel that?" he said, his voice low and seductive.

"Yes," she replied, her response barely above a whisper.

"Lesson number one. This is what happens to a man when you make him desire you."

She nodded, heat flooding her even further at the thought that she could cause such a reaction within him.

"Lesson number two?" he said, "is how I can make you feel."

He was lying on his side next to her, leaving her open and bare to him. He cupped her face once more before running his hand down her neck, over her collarbone, down her sternum until his fingers were caressing her stomach, and then over her chemise where she was open and waiting for him. He quickly left the area to continue down until he reached the hem.

He inched it upward, his palm rough against the softness of her legs as she waited for him.

"How does that feel?" he asked in a low tone.

"Good," she said, breathy with anticipation until his hand came between her legs.

He stroked her with his fingers, his thumb brushing against her entrance, causing her to shiver yet open her legs wider.

It was strange at first, to have him touch her so intimately, but as he continued, she warmed to his touch, allowing sensations of pleasure to wave over her.

"You like that," he stately smugly, and she opened one eye to look up at his smirk of satisfaction.

"I do," she said, keeping a note of annoyance in her tone at the fact he was so pleased with himself.

"Perfect," he said, "for we are just getting started."

With each stroke, his touch strengthened, and then his fingers were sliding inside of her, causing her to cry out in pleasure. He continued his explorations as he delved deeper, finding a place within her that she couldn't have led him to if she had tried.

Eliza moaned softly, her body arching into his touch, her hips moving in rhythm with his strokes. She was shocked and amazed at the sensations coursing through her, and still, she felt that her body was searching for something more, a release that she was desperate for.

"Fitz," she cried out as he leaned over and took her lips with his, making love to her mouth in time with his fingers thrusting inside of her. When his teeth nipped her bottom lip, it was enough to send her flying over the edge.

It was like nothing Eliza had ever felt before, nor anything she could ever have imagined. A wave of pure ecstasy washed over her entire body, her moans mingling with Fitz's groan as she realized, in thoughts that were outside of her body, that he seemed to enjoy this as much as she did.

She kept her eyes closed tightly as the intensity of the pleasure eventually subsided, leaving her weak and boneless, her body shaking from the aftershocks as she wondered how she was ever going to be able to stand up and walk away from him.

She could sense Fitz watching her, but she was unsure how she would ever look at him again after how she had just come completely apart in front of him.

"You did well," he whispered in her ear, his voice filled with admiration, causing her eyes to fly open.

"Is this what it is always like?" she asked, to which he grinned.

"With me? Yes. I can't make any promises for other men."

She snorted at that until she felt his hardness pressing against her, and she realized then that this was only the beginning. There was more to come.

So much more.

He took her hand and pulled her up, guiding her into a sitting position.

"How was that?"

"That was..." she paused, not wanting to stroke his ego,

but she also wanted more of this, and she supposed the truth was the best way to start. "Amazing."

"Good," he said, that cheeky grin crossing his face.

"Is there a lesson three?" she asked. While she wasn't sure that her body would be able to handle anymore, it could certainly give. She knew enough from her books to be aware that this could be a two-way event.

When she met his eyes, they were dark and full of lust, but he shook his head. "That should be enough for you today."

Disappointment ran through her.

"Is there nothing I can do for you?"

"That isn't what this is about," he said with a frown.

"These are lessons, Fitz," she said, looking up at him from beneath her lashes. "I wanted to experience pleasure, but I'd also like to give it."

She looked up at him with what she hoped was a convincing smile. "Please?"

He sighed, rolling his eyes up to the sky.

"Do you ever take no for an answer?" he said, but there was no malice to his tone. In fact, he seemed rather excited.

"Not really," she said, grinning.

"Very well," he said with what she knew was supposed to be a sigh of resignation, but he was clearly not too put out by the thought.

"Lesson number three it is."

CHAPTER 9

This woman was either going to be the death of him or bring him to a higher form of pleasure than he had ever known before.

At this point, however, he was willing to sacrifice himself.

"Should I put my mouth on you?" she asked with enthusiasm, and he had to do all he could to hold his groan within.

"While I would love that more than I can properly put into words," he said as sweat beaded on his brow, "let's start with something a bit simpler." He reached toward her. "Give me your hand."

She did as he requested, her complete trust nearly breaking him as he placed it on his member and then lay down before her as she had done to him. She stroked him lightly, sending his every nerve on edge.

"What do I do?"

Realizing he would hardly be able to form words, he placed his hand over hers, gripping it with just the right tightness before moving it up and down, from his base to the tip.

"Yes," he moaned as she continued, and soon enough she had the rhythm and he was able to release his hand, allowing her to continue on her own. What she lacked in inexperience she made up for with her effort, and Fitz wondered if there had ever been a more willing woman.

Fitz wanted to enjoy this and hoped it would last.

But it seemed her eagerness was far too much for him.

Fitz bit back a groan as his body tensed, the familiar sensation building up inside of him. He glanced down at Eliza's hand, still moving up and down over his shaft as he neared his breaking point.

His eyes closed briefly, as he desperately tried to extend the pleasure, but he could still picture the curve of her lips, her flushed cheeks, and the way her muscles rippled beneath her skin as she moved her hand. He relinquished himself to all of the sensations, lost in her, so caught up in her presence that he barely noticed the time passing.

A soft moan escaped his lips, and he gripped the linen beneath him tightly. His body filled with heat, and her scent surrounded him, a heady mixture of her perfume and perspiration. He could feel the inevitable cresting closer with every stroke of her hand, and he knew he had to stop her before he shocked her.

"Eliza," he murmured, his eyes flying open and meeting hers. She was watching her movements with a small smile of satisfaction on her face. "Stop now."

"Stop?" she said, sitting backward, her eyes widening. "Why?"

"Because I... I'm going to come, and I don't want to..."

"Come, then," she said, challenging him.

"But—"

It was too late, however. There was no more time to warn her away and soon enough he was finishing. He expected her to pull away, to be disgusted or, at the very least, shocked, but not Eliza. No, she just continued, pumping him until he finished and could do nothing more but lay his head back on the linen behind him.

"I'm sorry," he murmured, his eyes still closed, not wanting to look at her.

"For what?" she said, rustling around him, and when he finally had the strength to push himself up on his elbows, it was to watch her clean her hands in the lake, wipe them on the linen, and then begin to dress once more – as though this was something she did every day.

"For making a mess all over you."

"Easy enough to clean," she said cheerily. "Besides, I asked for it." She stopped, turning around to look at him over her shoulder. "Could you please lace up my dress?"

He wiped a hand over his face and pushed himself to his feet. "Of course."

He laced up the back of her dress, his fingers strangely shaking as he fastened the buttons before cleaning up himself and beginning to dress.

"Are you finished swimming?" she asked, and he nodded, as his very reason for swimming in the cold lake was standing before him.

"We should probably return to the house separately," he said. "You go first."

"Very well." She placed a few more pins in her hair. "Thank you, Fitz. I can't wait to do that again. Well, that… and more."

With one last cheeky grin, she sauntered off through the trees toward the house, leaving Fitz standing there in shock, wondering just what he had gotten himself into.

It was either the best decision he had ever made… or the worst.

**

Eliza had been a fool.

She'd read one book – *one* – about the intimacies that

could occur between men and women and suddenly she had thought she was some kind of expert.

An encounter with Fitz was all it had taken to prove that she knew nothing at all.

Until now.

After they had taken their pleasure, completely naked in the middle of the woods, she rushed back to the house as though she was being chased.

For she had been afraid that if she'd stayed, she would be unable to prevent herself from asking for more.

It was one thing to experiment.

It was another to become a complete wanton.

For the remainder of the day, she had been unable to think of anything else but Fitz, what he had done to her, and how he had made her feel. Now, she wanted nothing more but to do it again.

She wished she hadn't run off like she did, but rather had discussed with him when they would next meet. Now, she had no idea what she was supposed to do. Was she to proposition him again? If she waited for him to ask first, would she be waiting forever? She could only imagine all of the experienced lovers he had taken in the past. He was probably laughing to himself right now over how inexperienced and ineffective she was.

Eliza shook her head abruptly. It wasn't like her to question herself. Damn it, but she did do a good job. He had finished, had he not?

If it was with anyone else, she knew it would be no issue, that she would be as certain of herself as she always was.

But this was Fitz. The man who ignored her, who she was sure had still seen her as a young girl, whose eyes had passed over her every time he came upon her in the ballroom unless he was forced to dance with her because her brother had struck some deal.

She flung herself back on her bed, awaiting her lady's maid to come attend to her for dinner.

A dinner in which she would likely have to sit at the same table as Fitz and pretend that nothing had happened between them.

She desperately wished that she had someone she could ask for advice. If only Siena was here. But no, Siena was happily married, hours away, and completely unaware of any of the dynamics between Fitz and Eliza.

Goodness, she wished that she had told Siena of the history between the two of them. Or *lack* of history as one would have it. That she'd had such a penchant for him. That she was the only lady Lord Fitzroy did not see as a woman.

Until she had practically forced him to.

She sat bolt upright in bed.

She might not be able to sit down and have the conversation with Siena that she longed to have, but she could still tell her all about her plight.

Deciding that dinner and her maid could wait for a time, she jumped off the bed, seeking out the library, where there was sure to be stationary. Appleton claimed a smaller library, but from what she could remember, it was quiet, comfortable, and contained a small writing desk that looked over the sash windows into the beautiful, blooming garden below and the orchard that sat in the distance.

Eliza pulled out the ornate, elegant chair, laughing to herself at the idea of Fitz sitting in it, before finding stationary. She dipped her quill into the ink and began to write, pouring her heart out on the page, telling Siena all that she should have shared with her before now.

She was careful in wording her arrangement with Fitz. While Siena would never betray her secrets, there was always the chance a letter could fall into the wrong hands.

A crush was one thing. A scandalous affair was another.

But she would have to risk it. She replaced the pen and

folded her letter, finding a stamp and wax in the desk drawer. Once she was certain that her private letter was sealed, she carefully wrote Siena's new address on the outside before finding one of the servants to ask for it to be sent away immediately.

Maybe Siena would be able to respond in time with answers.

One could only hope, for at the moment Eliza, the woman who claimed to know everything, was completely and utterly lost.

* * *

FITZ HAD AVOIDED dinner the previous evening.

Not on purpose – in truth, he did have business to attend to – but he didn't think he had it within him to stare at Eliza all evening, knowing what was hiding beneath her gown.

Full, luscious breasts.

Hips that he could take hold of and use to his advantage.

Soft skin, dotted with the tiniest of dark freckles.

Whether she hated him or not, her body had certainly welcomed him, and he wondered when would be too soon to ask her to meet him for their next lesson.

He grew hard just thinking about what that lesson would be.

That afternoon, the day after their liaison, he was back in his study, seeing to various matters of the estate. He threw a letter into the pile to be posted and then saw that his mother's letters were sitting on his desk, waiting to be franked.

Deciding he deserved a break, he reached over and began to initial them – until he realized that the letter he was holding in his hand was not his mother's handwriting at all. It was much firmer, with broad, loopy strokes, nothing at all like his mother's delicate script.

He held the letter in his hand, seeing the seal as well as Dunmore's wife's name on the outside. It was from Eliza.

He shifted the letter from one hand to the next.

He shouldn't. This was Eliza's private letter, written for her friend alone.

And yet... he wondered, just what did she have to say that was so important she had to write her friend immediately? Would she dare to put anything about their arrangement on paper?

It was one thing to have a dalliance with a widow or a lady who was not of high birth. It was quite another to do so with a young lady who would one day be expected to enter her marriage completely innocent. If she told anyone...

That settled it. He best open it and discover just what she had said. He could always re-seal it.

He cracked the letter open, finding that it was one written page, from Eliza to Siena, who was now married to the Duke of Dunmore, his closest friend in the world.

And oh, what an intriguing letter it appeared to be.

He sat back in his chair, crossed one leg over the other as he rested them on the desk, and began to read.

My dearest Siena,

I am so sorry to disturb you and the duke. You were correct in sensing that there was more between me and Lord Fitzroy, and I only wish I had confided in you before I left. You had battled through so much that I did not want to add any more concerns to your list.

But let me first tell you why any of this matters.

She proceeded to explain how she had come to be at Fitz's estate, as well as the fact that most of his sisters had left his country home to visit friends.

As you know, I have been acquainted with Lord Fitzroy for some time, being friends with his sisters. When I was a girl, I so fancied him.

Interesting.

Not, of course, that I ever expected him to see me in return. He was quite a few years older than me, and usually away at school. When we did encounter one another, I am sure he looked at me as a young girl.

That much was true.

Then I came of age. I knew he would be at my first outing, and while I never expected anything to come of it, nor did I hold my childish penchant for him any longer. However, I had still hoped that he would notice me.

He didn't even look my way.

On that, she was wrong.

Instead, he spent the rest of the night charming every other debutante, danced with each of them, and likely went home with one of the widows who had been eyeing him all night.

Wrong again – on the widow part, at least.

When the night came to a close, he came to collect his sisters, who I was standing with. You were being charmed by some overly eager young lord, likely politely turning him away. When Lord Fitzroy finally looked at me, it was only to say goodnight, and, Siena, I am sorry to say that I allowed my outspoken spirit to take over and I was rather rude to him.

Fitz smiled wide when he read that. She had been rude. He would never forget how she had spoken to him – "You, Lord Fitzroy, can take your goodnight and place it where—" She had stopped before she had reached the end, but it had certainly left an impression on him, even as he had wondered all of these years later just what he had done to deserve her derision. Now he knew.

I saw him time and again afterward, but it was always the same. He went out of his way to avoid me, and I realized that despite other suitors showing interest in me, there must be something wrong with me. *The man loves everything that moves with breasts — what was it about me that turned him away?*

If only she knew.

It caused great ire within me, and I must say that I have never been overly agreeable to Lord Fitzroy. It was why I was annoyed with him when he appeared at Greystone at the same time I did. I had no choice but to be polite — as was he, when he was forced into proximity with me.

I am sure we would have lived the rest of our days crossing paths politely had I not arrived here at Appleton.

I was bored, Siena. It is my only excuse. Between my boredom and my goal to obtain experiences that I had only before read about, I asked him if he would help.

I didn't give him much choice in the matter, I'm afraid.

Fitz laughed out loud at that.

He agreed to partner with me to learn about the various matters that I have told you about that arose in the book of Baxter's I found.

The cheeky little minx, stealing her brother's book. His chuckle continued.

When we finished our first session, I left. Walked away. Now, I have no idea if he is truly interested, or just humoring me. Did I make a mistake? Oh, Siena, I wish you were here to tell me what to do.

I hope you are enjoying your time with your husband.

I love you always!

Eliza

FITZ SET the letter down in front of him, steepling his fingers underneath his chin. So, she was under the impression he thought there was something wrong with her, then, did she?

Well, now that he had this information, he would have to show her that so many of her assumptions were in error.

Except for one — that she had made the right choice in propositioning him.

CHAPTER 10

"I must have this meeting, Mother. If it is not safe enough for me to go to London, then these men will come here to me. They shall not be here long, and then they will be on their way again."

"I do not mind hosting, Fitz, but will it not be odd, without women to balance out the numbers?"

"Perhaps, but it is just for a night. I meet with these gentlemen, sign some documents, host the dinner, and then they will be gone the next day. Easy."

Eliza peeked around the corner. She shouldn't be listening to Fitz's conversation with his mother, but she had been passing by his study when she had heard their voices within. When she heard "hosting" she had been interested, and she paused outside the door, just out of sight.

"I wish your sisters were here," Lady Fitzroy sighed.

"No, you do not," Fitz countered. "There is no need for them to be in the house with unattached men. The only socializing will be during the dinner hour. The rest will be purely Parliamentry business."

"Very well," his mother said. "I suppose it will be exciting for the staff." And for Lady Fitzroy, Eliza imagined, although she didn't admit it. "When will they arrive?"

"Noon."

"What day?"

"Today."

"Today! Fitz, how long have you known?"

"Since we left London. But I didn't want you to fret, so I never said anything."

"But the Cook—"

"I already told her, and the butler," Fitz said. "Nothing to worry about."

"Oh dear." Eliza could practically hear Lady Fitzroy wringing her hands. "I shall have to go tell Lady Willoughby."

"Lady Willoughby loves company. I do not think it should be an issue. Plus, it is your house. You can do as you want, no matter what Lady Willoughby thinks."

"Yes, but—"

"Thank you, Mother," he said firmly. "I promise that you shall barely know they are here."

"Very well," she said, beginning to back out of the room, and Eliza scrambled away, glad for the carpeted runner over the floor and her kid slippers, which prevented her from making any noise.

When she turned around, however, pretending that she had just turned into the foyer, she didn't miss Fitz's expression as he watched her, one eyebrow raised as though he knew exactly what she was doing.

She lifted her chin, telling herself to stand strong as she marched by him down the hallway.

"Good morning, Lord Fitzroy," she said, hoping she sounded normal. "Lady Fitzroy."

"Good morning, Lady Eliza," his mother said, joining her to walk toward the drawing room, where Eliza knew her mother awaited. "I hope you are having a nice stay."

Eliza continued to chatter but couldn't help looking behind her at Fitz. His eyes seemed to be burning a hole in her back, and a tremor of anticipation raced through her.

Forward or not, she was going to have to approach him again.

Unless... an idea began to form in her mind. One that had her lips curling up in glee.

Fitz had agreed to this with her only when she had suggested that she would find another to take on the role instead.

Perhaps she could work this political visit to her advantage.

* * *

As it turned out, Eliza didn't have it within her to contrive any games.

She had dressed in one of her favorite gowns that evening – a deep rose, one that her mother had suggested she should have ordered in a lighter shade, but Eliza had insisted that she far preferred the more jewel tone.

Flowers were softly inlaid along the hem of the gown, with blush pink ribbon lacing the bodice and the sleeves.

She hoped that Fitz's friends might notice her, making it easier to flirt with them, but deep within, she knew the truth – that the only one she cared about noticing her was Fitz.

Betsy and Daphne, Fitz's youngest sisters, remained upstairs with the governess when the gentlemen arrived, leaving Lady Fitzroy, Lady Willoughby, and Eliza to greet the visitors along with Fitz.

The two gentlemen arrived on horses, creating quite the dashing pair as they rode up Appleton's drive. Eliza turned to whisper to one of her friends what she thought of them but realized quickly she was alone. Strange, for her. She sighed, catching Fitz's attention, as he turned to look sharply at her.

"Something the matter?" he asked, with that crooked eyebrow that had more expression in it than most men held within their entire face.

"Not at all," she said, forcing her lips into the most demure smile she could manage. He continued to stare at her suspiciously, but she simply shrugged as she considered this the beginning of her plan.

"Fitz!" one of the gentlemen called out as they neared. "You've made a few simple signatures rather difficult for us."

"Could have sent a clerk or secretary," he responded, a wide grin splitting his face, reminding Eliza of who he was and how much he meant to so many people who also had demands on his time.

"Ah, we've missed you, Fitz," the other tall, bearded blond man said. "We also appear to be the lucky ones as you have greeted us with such beautiful ladies."

That earned a blush from Lady Fitzroy and Lady Willoughby, each of whom laughed and waved him off, while Eliza wanted to roll her eyes. Another charmer. She was pleased, however, for this could work in her favor.

After handing off the reins of their horses, the two gentlemen ascended the stairs. Eliza recognized the first, a dark-haired man with a severe hairstyle, long sideburns, and angular features.

"Lord Whitby," she said with a curtsy when it was her turn to greet him. "It is good to see you."

"And you, Lady Eliza," he said. "How is your brother?"

"He is... as prolific as ever," she said with a grin, which had Fitz snorting beside her, although he covered it with a cough.

"I see," Lord Whitby said politely, while he didn't appear to understand why the other man wore a smirk.

"I do not believe we have had the pleasure," said the second man who Fitz introduced as Lord Brighton. "I am *very* pleased to make your acquaintance, Lady Eliza."

He took her hand, bowing over it before placing a soft kiss on her glove. Eliza's eyes widened as Fitz practically bristled beside her. She smiled broadly. She didn't have to play the game at all.

Truth be told, while these gentlemen should be as ideal candidates as any, whether it be for courtship, for attention, or even for her grand experiment itself, there was no plan for her to design.

They were handsome, they were charming, they were well respected.

But they did not seem to capture her attention as Fitz did.

Which was as disconcerting as anything.

Perhaps her intentions tonight had been ill-conceived. Perhaps, instead of trying to cause Fitz to notice her as a woman, she should see if she could convince herself to bestow her attention on another. A man who wasn't Fitz. Who she wasn't at risk of losing her heart to.

"Shall we go in?" Fitz asked, irritation lacing his usually jovial voice. When they all agreed, Lord Brighton offered Eliza his arm, which she quickly took, leaving Fitz to escort her mother in and Lord Whitby with Lady Willoughby.

"Fitz, before we go in, I have some news to share," Lord Brighton said, unease on his face.

"Out with it, Brighton."

"Lord Mandrake is also on his way."

"What?" Fitz exclaimed so loudly that his mother jumped.

"It couldn't be helped," Brighton said, shrugging, holding his hands out in supplication as Fitz looked toward Lord Whitby for obvious assistance. "He's on this committee and didn't trust us to do this without him."

"Boll—" Fitz began, but then looked toward the women watching him before sighing and running his hand through his hair. "Why didn't he accompany you?"

"He said he had business to attend to first and would be

coming from another of his estates." Lord Brighton peered into the distance. "I believe he is on his way now."

"Fitz," his mother said in obvious warning. "We will welcome him as we would anyone else."

"Fine," Fitz said, rubbing a spot in the middle of his forehead. "But keep the girls upstairs. Thank goodness Dot isn't here."

Eliza must ask Fitz why he hated the man so much. Lord Mandrake wasn't the most pleasant of men, to be sure, but he wasn't the worst she had ever met.

Mandrake had ridden down the drive toward them, as Fitz awaited with his arms crossed over his chest.

"Mandrake," he intoned.

"Ah, the warm welcome I was expecting," Mandrake said with ire.

"Well, when a man shows up uninvited—"

"I believe that we will leave you to your business," his mother cut in, likely to prevent any animosities from spilling over.

"Very well. We shall conduct our meetings for a few hours before convening for dinner," Fitz said. "We shall see you ladies then."

They said farewell before Eliza followed her mother and Lady Fitzroy into the drawing room. She had only just taken a seat when she noticed that both women were leaning forward from the sofa, staring at her.

"What is it?" she asked, instantly lifting a hand to rub at her cheeks. "Do I have cream on my face?" She had stolen a cream puff from a tray earlier and had hoped that no one would notice.

"Eliza, I believe Lord Brighton is rather taken by you," her mother said, her chest puffing out with pride.

Eliza waved a hand in the air. "I doubt it," she said. "He was simply being charming."

"In the times that I have been in his acquaintance, I have

never seen him so interested in any young lady before, including my daughters," Lady Fitzroy said.

"Here I worried about leaving London at a time when you should be finding a husband," her mother said. "Little did I know that all we had to do was come to Essex with Lord Fitzroy!"

Eliza's laugh was forced as she wondered what her mother would say if she knew the truth of what had happened between her and Lord Fitzroy – and what she hoped would happen again soon.

The late afternoon became evening, the time passing slower than Eliza would have liked, but soon enough the men appeared, tiredness in their eyes as they led the ladies into dinner, Eliza once again accompanying Lord Brighton. Lord Mandrake followed them all unescorted, although he didn't seem to mind.

She didn't miss Fitz's eyes on her, and truth be told, she could hardly tear hers away from him. Lord Brighton was chatting in her ear, and she smiled and nodded as though she was listening to every word that came out of his mouth, but the truth was, she was having a difficult time concentrating when Fitz was walking in front of her.

All she could concentrate on was the way his muscular thighs filled out his breeches, how the pants cupped his buttocks, how broad his shoulders were in relation to the rest of him, and how his strong fingers reminded her of the magic they could work.

She was so caught up that she nearly walked into the back of her mother when she and Fitz stopped abruptly in front of her.

"Let's see," Lady Fitzroy said, a gleam in her eye. "Lady Eliza, why do you not sit here beside Lord Brighton?" she said, pointing to the opposite end of the table from where Fitz had taken a seat.

"They can sit here," Fitz said, pointing beside him so that Eliza would be on his left.

"Very well," Lady Fitzroy said with an interested glance at her son. "We shall switch, then."

Lord Brighton *was* rather entertaining. He had known Fitz for quite some time, and he enjoyed telling stories about their exploits together, although Eliza was sure that these were only tame stories because of the presence of ladies. Lord Mandrake sat next to Lord Whitby, silent and sullen, obviously understanding that he was not entirely welcome here. Lord Whitby didn't have the stories Lord Brighton did, and when he did have the opportunity to speak, he droned on and on until Eliza nearly fell asleep.

They must have opened up the liquor cabinet because from what Eliza could tell, Lord Brighton's tongue was a lot looser than it should have been in their company. Not that she minded, for she was quite enjoying the stories, her attention captured.

The only thing that was distracting her was the pressure of Fitz's leg against hers. She had no idea whether he was doing it on purpose or if he thought that she was part of the table, but she had to admit she kind of liked it.

Lord Brighton took another sip of the port that seemed to be magically refilling due to the diligence of the footman behind him.

"Then, there was one time at school when Fitz and I wagered to see which one of us could set a particular garment waving on the flagpole. I thought for certain that I could win this one, but Fitz went out of his way to become the victor. He—"

"I think that's enough," Fitz said firmly, putting his drink down on the table in front of him.

"Oh, but we were just getting to the good part," Lord Brighton said before Lord Whitby chimed in, "probably best not to tell that story in the company of the ladies."

"Ah," Lord Brighton said, sitting back in his seat as though he had forgotten just who he was sitting with. Eliza supposed that could be forgiven since the three women who were present were not exactly the most proper of ladies to have ever made his acquaintance.

"I don't mind," Eliza said, knowing that she was probably pushing it too far, but she had an indescribable need to learn more of what lengths Fitz had gone to. She had a feeling it involved a woman. Why she wanted more information about Fitz with another woman, she had no idea, but it was like some perverse need to know more.

"You should," Fitz said, but that wasn't what caused her to stop talking. It was his hand, which had come under the table and gripped her thigh.

Gripped it high enough to have her swallowing hard in surprise.

"Lord Whitby, why do you not tell us about your land?" Lady Fitzroy said. "I hear that you came into an unexpected inheritance recently."

"Why, yes, I did," Lord Whitby said as he began rambling on, only Eliza couldn't have repeated anything he spoke about.

She was far too focused on Fitz's hand.

And the way it was moving up her leg.

CHAPTER 11

Fitz was playing with fire.

But then, so was Eliza. Watching her sit next to Brighton, a smile on her face as she listened to his stories, was placing him closer to the edge than he liked.

What edge that was, he wasn't sure, but he felt about ready to combust between his ire as well as his need to have Eliza beneath him again.

It was as if her every movement, her every word, her every damn breath was calling to him, making him want her more intensely than he had ever wanted another before.

Somewhere in the back of his mind where the rational thought lived, he knew that part of the reason she was so enjoying Brighton's stories was because they were about him, but he still had this intense, sudden need to possess all of her smiles, to protect them with another.

So, he decided it was time to have his own bit of fun.

He took possession of her thigh, inching his fingers upward, enjoying watching her face as she tried to hide her reaction to him.

There was the initial widening of her eyes, which was soon followed by the swallow, causing movement in the long column of her throat, and then the forced smile to hide what she was truly feeling.

But not once did she bring her hand down to cover his, nor give him any hint that she wanted him to stop. Which made him want her all the more. He ran his fingers over the silky fabric of her dress. He should know what material it was, having seven sisters, but truth be told, he didn't overly care if it was silk, satin, or muslin. It made no difference to him.

What he cared most about was that it was draped over her body, hugging her curves, hiding that beautiful skin from him.

It was soft, that was for certain, and welcomed his fingers as they ran over it until they reached the crease where her leg began. He lightly danced his fingers over her center before leaving it again, doused in satisfaction when she practically jumped.

"Are you well, Lady Eliza?" Lord Whitby said, interrupting his recitation of his lands to peer closely at her.

"Just fine," she said, her voice practically a squeak, and Fitz had to hide his smile behind his other hand as the man continued.

He wished he could find a way through this fabric to actually touch her, but there was no recourse for that – not here, not now.

There was only one thing to do about it – get everyone to bed and hope that he could find his way to her bedroom without anyone noticing him.

The question was whether either of them would make it until that time. She was biting her lip now, a slight sheen of perspiration shining on her forehead.

Fitz began rubbing faster, the muscles in his hand tightening as he kept his arm as still as possible so his actions wouldn't be obvious.

"Eliza, I say, you are looking rather peaked," her mother

said, and when Eliza nodded, Fitz had to bite down on the inside of his cheek to keep from smiling, although he decided he should best take pity on her and he stopped, finally allowing her peace. He thought she would be relieved, but her brow only tightened.

He had a fairly good idea why.

"You are right, Mother. I believe I am simply tired. I would not like to ruin the night, but I believe I should go lie down," she said, fanning her face with one hand.

Fitz liked the sound of that.

"I should come with you," her mother said, pushing back her chair.

"No!" Eliza exclaimed before softening her voice. "That is, I am fine. Thank you, Mother."

"Very well," her mother said. "If you do need me, though, please send someone for me."

"Of course," Eliza said, beginning to push out her chair. Brighton tried to stand, but the copious amount of port he had consumed slowed his actions, and Fitz was proud of himself for standing quickly enough to beat Brighton to help her.

"Allow me," he said, pulling back her chair, surreptitiously running his fingers over the bare skin of her neck, noting her shiver.

"Good night, everyone," she said, nodding at them as she walked out of the room.

Fitz waited but a moment before he tapped on his chin and said, "You know, I have a bottle of wine that I have been meaning to try for some time and this seems like the perfect occasion."

The footman nodded at him and made to leave, but Fitz held up a hand. "I have it saved somewhere special. I shall go myself to find the exact bottle. Please excuse me for one moment," he said, before walking out of the room as fast as he could, pleased to find that Eliza hadn't gone far. She turned around when he shut the door to the dining room.

"Fitz," she hissed as she strode up to him. "You—"

"Come with me," he murmured, and she blinked up at him, her big blue eyes so wide that he nearly lost himself in their depths.

"Where?"

"Do you trust me?"

"No."

He laughed softly. "Come with me anyway?"

"Fine," she said warily, and he took her hand, leading her through the room to the other side so that no one could see them from the drawing room.

He led her through the breakfast room, into the kitchen and down a flight of stairs which she was sure were for the servants. Before rounding the corner at the bottom, he stopped her, placing a finger against her lips as he peeked around the corner to find that only the cook was present, her back to them. Fitz tilted his head and Eliza followed him, understanding the need for silence.

Fortunately, the door he was interested in was unlocked, likely due to its use during the dinner hour, and soon enough they entered the cool, dark room filled floor to ceiling with wine casks.

He appreciated the coolness of the wine cellar, for he had become rather heated upstairs. He turned to Eliza, barely able to see her in the dim light, and yet her features seemed to have been imprinted in his mind.

"What are we doing?" she whispered, and he hauled her toward him.

"I couldn't wait any longer. The butler's pantry held too many delicate items and our bedrooms were too far away," he said, surprised by the desperation in his voice.

"Wait for what?"

"For you," he said as he fiercely took her lips, claiming her as he had wanted to upstairs when Lord Brighton had looked upon her with such admiration.

He stepped her backward until she was pressed against the thick stone behind her, an oak table in the corner set up for wine tasting catching his eye. A lone flickering candle, obviously left by the butler who had been selecting their drinks for the evening, cast dancing shadows on the walls, adding a touch of mystery to the intimate setting.

Fitz's hands roamed over Eliza's curves with a hunger that had been building all evening. Her skin was silk beneath his fingertips, which longed for more.

Eliza's breath hitched beneath his lips as her fingers stroked his chest, over far more layers than he would have liked.

The scent of aged wine, mixed with the heady aroma of desire, surrounded them. Their kisses grew deeper, more urgent, each one a promise of their unfolding passion.

Fitz swiveled her around and backed her toward the table before sweeping his arm across its surface, sending the ledger and a wine glass clattering to the floor. Fitz lowered himself to lift Eliza, sitting her on the edge of the table, her knees spread wide so that he could fit between them and trail urgent kisses along her jawline and down her neck.

She gasped, clutching his shoulders as he explored every inch of her delicate skin with fervor. Her taste was like a fine vintage wine, intoxicating and unforgettable.

Fitz deftly unfastened the laces of her gown one by one until the fabric fell away, revealing the creamy expanse of her bare skin. Eliza's chest rose and fell rapidly as she arched into his touch in a silent plea for more.

Fitz took a moment to appreciate her ample breasts, cupping them before tracing his tongue around each nipple, appreciating how they responded to him.

"Fitz," Eliza moaned, his name on her lips only spurring him on further.

Fitz's hands moved with purpose, skimming up her thighs beneath the fabric of her gown. Eliza's breath quickened as he inched the fabric higher, exposing her skin to his hungry gaze.

Fitz's lips found hers in a fervent kiss, his desire for her palpable in every stroke of his tongue.

He leaned back from her, their eyes locking as the realization swept over them that there was no turning back once they took the next step forward.

"Is this lesson four?" Eliza asked breathlessly.

Fitz chuckled hoarsely. "I think we're skipping right over a few lessons," he said. "Unless you'd rather not."

"Oh, I'd rather," she said. "I'd rather very much."

He sucked in a ragged breath as he was overcome, not by the passion between them but by how much he appreciated this woman and her forthright ways. He did not need to wonder or question when she had no qualms about telling him exactly what she wanted and needed.

And the fact that it was *him* she needed right now? Well, that was more than he could ever want.

No longer able to contain themselves, they eagerly undid the remaining fastenings on their clothes, and their breath quickened in unison at the anticipation of what was to come.

Fitz didn't miss Eliza's shaking hands as she unfastened the buttons of his trousers, revealing the hard evidence of his desire.

She gazed upon him, eyes wide and aroused, the flickering candlelight dancing in their depths. Her gaze mirrored his hunger, racing his heart even faster.

Their lips met once more with a fierceness that made them both gasp for breath. As their tongues danced and mingled, their fingers explored the curves and hollows of each other's bodies.

Fitz's hand moved to the small of Eliza's back, pulling her closer to him, his heart pounding in rhythm with hers. He kept his touch feather-light, dancing over the delicate skin at the back of her neck, her shiver as he played her body with his touch causing a sense of pride within him.

He slid his hands down her sides, grazing her hips and then reaching around to cup her bottom. She moaned softly, arching into him, and as much as Fitz wanted to savor this moment, he also knew that he couldn't wait any longer.

He lifted her gown, sliding it onto the table beside them as best he could, bunching the rest around her waist. He wished that he could have her completely bare beneath him, but their time was limited, and he would have to take what he could get.

He slid his hands up her silky thighs until he found the very center of her, running his fingers over her before sliding them inside, making sure that she was ready for him.

He found there were no concerns to be had there.

"Are you ready for me, Eliza?" he asked once more, needing to know.

"Yes, Fitz, please," she cried out, her fingers digging into his shoulders.

Holding her close, taking her lips with his, he notched himself against her, and with one powerful thrust, sent himself home.

CHAPTER 12

*E*liza's breath left her body in a whoosh.

For a moment, she wondered whether her mind and body were still connected. It was pleasure and pain, all wrapped up together, and Fitz stilled against her, as though sensing her discomfort.

She wrapped her arms around his shoulders, holding him close against her, trying to draw strength from him to make it through this moment.

"Eliza, are you all right?" he asked, his voice nearly unrecognizable, so choked it was with desire, and she nodded against him.

"I just need a moment."

"Take all that the time you need."

She breathed deeply a few times, allowing her body to become used to him. Concentrating instead on his breath, hot on her cheek, and his hard body against her, she was finally able to relax, surprised that when she did so the pain receded, leaving only the pleasure behind.

Pleasure and some uncertainty, but she supposed that was part of the adventure.

"I'm ready," she said hoarsely.

"Tell me if you want me to stop," he said.

"I will."

He began moving within her, thrusts that began soft and slow, gradually increasing in speed and intensity until she found herself moving against him as well, seeking that pinnacle she had received from him before and so longed for again.

The table was cool beneath her thighs, so at odds with her heated body, and as Fitz rocked faster, the table began to move as well until the front legs were coming off the floor with his every movement.

Eliza held onto him tightly, needing him as her anchor of support, and he held her fast against him, not letting her go.

The build-up of the entire evening seemed to have only spiraled her need for him out of control, the thrill of doing this in such a forbidden place increasing her excitement, and soon enough she found herself reaching that edge once more, spiraling around him.

"Eliza," she heard Fitz say in the distance, but she was so caught up in her need to fall over the precipice of her desire that she didn't acknowledge him, only holding him tighter against her as she needed him to stay exactly where he was, to allow her pleasure to reach its fulfillment.

"Eliza, I need to—" Fitz's words broke off with a shout as he began to still against her, his only movements a shuddery jerk that told her he was coming along with her, his pulsing in synch with hers.

She couldn't have said how long it went on for, only that all she could hear was their intermingled breath – until she became more aware of a dim sound beyond them. A knock.

They both jumped, Fitz whispering a curse, "Oh, shit," as he slid out of her and began to fasten his breeches as quickly as he could before reaching out to help her reassemble her clothing.

"My lord? Are you within?" came a voice from beyond,

one that Eliza didn't recognize but Fitz whispered, "The butler," before looking frantically around them.

"Yes, I am here," he said, making Eliza swivel her head toward him, for how was she supposed to explain her presence here? "I seem to have locked myself in."

"One moment, my lord. I need to find the key and then I will have you out of here shortly."

The jingling of keys only sent Eliza's already frazzled nerves on edge, and Fitz hissed, "Hide," as he lifted her off of the table and pulled her toward the far wall, gesturing toward a space at the bottom between the wine casks.

She opened her mouth, ready to tell him exactly what she thought of hiding in the dark corners of a damp wine cellar, but then the door began to open, and she had to act without further thought, cramming herself in the tight space, grateful, at least, for the dim light of the room.

"Apologies, my lord," the butler said, allowing light from the kitchen beyond into the room. "Your guests and your mother were becoming worried about your absence. Had I known you were here—"

"Not a problem at all, Hastings," Fitz said, his silhouette visible from Eliza's hiding space. He ran a hand over his hair, which was sticking up at odd angles after she had run her fingers through it so aggressively. "Thank you for rescuing me."

"Of course, my lord," the butler said, pausing for a moment. "Is all well?"

"Oh, yes," Fitz said, following Hastings' gaze toward the table, which was rather… askew. Even the candle had been knocked over, explaining why the room had been sent into such darkness. "I'm afraid I jostled the tasting table. I will arrange everything as it was."

"We will do that, my lord."

"No, no, now that I have light, I will find the drink in question and bring it up."

"Which is it? I will gather it for you."

"Hastings, I would prefer to do it myself. Sometimes I like to feel... useful, if you know what I am saying."

"Yes, my lord," Hastings said, even though he was obviously baffled by his lord's bizarre behavior. But if Fitz departed, it would likely mean she would be locked in here or left to be discovered by the staff.

"I will keep a wedge in the door so that you are not locked in again," the butler said before backing away.

"Thank you, Hastings," Fitz said, remaining where he was until the butler's retreating footsteps could be heard echoing away and Fitz rushed over to where she was crouched, stuck in the wine rack.

He reached his hands in and helped her out, as Eliza tried not to be cross with him. Her anger quickly fled, however, when she saw how distressed he was.

"Eliza, I am so sorry," he said, his forehead creased in worry. "I should never have—"

"It's fine," she said, waving away his words. "I didn't want to be caught in here either. Did I like hiding as though I should be ashamed? No. But I would have had no excuse for my presence here, had I been discovered."

"It's not that," he said, shaking his head urgently, and she stared at him closer, for she had never seen this side of Fitz before, such concern on his face, causing his entire body to hover on edge.

"Then what is it?"

A noise sounded from outside the room, and he shook his head, although his consternation remained.

"We don't have time to discuss now. I'll come to you tonight, all right?"

She nodded succinctly before he walked to the door, looking from one side to the next before motioning toward her, and she walked toward him, stopping when he grabbed her hand.

"When you get to your room, lock your door and do not allow anyone in except me, all right?"

"Why?" she couldn't help but ask, never one to do as she was told without question.

"I know these gentlemen are my visitors, but I do not entirely trust them," he said before pausing and saying with a frown, "not that I'm much better."

"The difference is, I wanted this with you," she said, placing a quick kiss on his lips and squeezing his hand quickly before slipping past him and up the stairs to find her chamber.

Grateful when she made it there unnoticed, she shut the door behind her and collapsed against it, sinking to the floor as she brought her hands to her chest, breathing deeply as all that had just occurred washed over her.

She had pictured this day for so long – making love to a man, feeling that immense sense of pleasure, and becoming a complete woman.

It was nothing like she could ever have imagined.

It was so much better.

* * *

HE SHOULD HAVE KNOWN BETTER. After his past, to allow this… well. He had to speak to Eliza – not that he could fix anything now. It was too late. All they could do was wait.

He had worried about how long it would take him to convince the other gentlemen to retire for the night.

Fortunately, his mother and Eliza's called the night to a close shortly after he reappeared, and Brighton's drunken state sent him to bed early. Fitz was sure that Whitby would have stayed up for hours and droned on about the most minute of circumstances, rehashing every word spoken in Parliament while Fitz had been away, but fortunately, Fitz had been able to make his excuses and soon depart.

His steps were heavy as he climbed the stairs, stopping in front of Eliza's bedchamber. He laid his head against the door, wondering how he was going to face her.

What he had done was inexcusable. While coming together with her had been one of – if not *the* – best moments of his life, he should never have released inside of her. He had no idea if she was even aware of what he had done or what it could mean for them.

He knocked on the door as quietly as he could, and she whipped it open as though she had been waiting for him.

He slipped inside, finding that she was already prepared for the night. He stepped toward her, sliding his hands over her shoulders and her bare upper arms. "Are you all right?" he asked, to which she frowned at him.

"Why wouldn't I be?"

"Well, after we—that is—"

"Fitz," she said, her lips sliding into the smile that he so loved, the dimples on her cheeks popping. "That was amazing. There is nothing to apologize for."

"But there is," he said, taking her hands and leading her over to the bed, sitting them both down upon the end of it. "I... I finished within you," he said, looking deeply into her eyes. "Do you know what that could mean?"

"Yes," she said, her lashes flicking downward to cover her gaze. "There is a chance – a slight chance – that it could put me with child. I know that. I am not stupid."

"I never said you were. But it was my fault. I should never have allowed myself to—"

She held up a hand. "It's done, Fitz," she said gently. "I suppose we shall find out in due time if anything will come of it. But there is nothing we can do now."

"I do not suppose there is."

She reached out, cupping his cheeks. "I like to think of all that could come of this. That was, to me, incredible. Do you know that?"

A rush of peace washed over him. If she could look at this with such positivity, then so could he.

"Absolutely," he said. "Incredible is a wonderful word for it."

"Do you think… we could do that again sometime?"

A laugh whooshed out of him. "In the wine cellar?"

She dropped her hands and shook her head, laughter lighting her eyes. "Maybe not the wine cellar. How about a bed?"

"I think that could be arranged."

"Good," she said with an impish smile. "You know where to find me, it seems."

"That I do," he said, pausing for a moment, wondering if he should tell her what he was thinking or if it would admit too much to her. "Tell me why you hated me."

He knew but wanted to hear it from her.

"I never hated you."

"You certainly acted like you did."

She sighed as she stood and began to take small steps back and forth in front of him, reminding him of himself and all of the pacing that he did.

"I'm not sure if I should admit this… but I had a bit of a penchant for you when I was young."

"Only when you were young?" he said teasingly, and she shot him a look of annoyance.

"I thought it had faded until I came out and you completely ignored me. I suppose there was always a part of me that was still interested in you, that wanted your approval if nothing else."

He stared at her, wondering how she couldn't realize how captivatingly beautiful she was.

"I noticed you," he said quietly.

She snorted. "You did not. You completely ignored me."

"That was on purpose."

"What are you talking about?"

"I noticed you and admired you far more than I should have. You were young, my sisters' friend, and..." he couldn't tell her that she was all wrong for him. He had no wish to hurt her. "... and I couldn't allow you to see how much I wanted you."

"So, you decided completely avoiding me was better?"

"I did." It sounded foolish when she put it like that.

"I—" she had stopped pacing as she gaped at him instead. "I'm not entirely sure what to say. I had no idea. I thought you looked at me as a young girl."

"Quite the opposite. I *should* have looked at you as a young girl. Instead, I saw a woman who was far too desirable."

"Well," she said with a sly grin, "It seems that your feelings worked to my advantage. If only we had discovered them all sooner."

He was already shaking his head. "Then I only would have been in greater trouble."

She crossed her arms over her chest as she tilted her head to study him. "Why do you feel I am so wrong for you?"

"What do you mean?" he said, trying not to answer her question, for he knew very well what she meant, but to answer her truthfully would only hurt her.

"I mean that I could be a suitable wife for you. We are both at the age when it is expected."

A flutter in his chest that was very akin to panic began to grow at the mention of the word *wife*. He had pushed the thought of marriage to the side for so long that even though he knew it was time he found a wife, actually putting a face and name to her was disconcerting – especially after the one time he had thought he would become a married man.

He couldn't imagine a wife more entertaining or enjoyable than Eliza, however. The only problem was she was not the kind of wife he needed. If he wanted to marry off his sisters and have any chance of the rest of the House taking him and his proposals seriously, he needed a respectable woman by his side. One who would sit demurely and entertain and say all of the right things.

But he couldn't very well tell Eliza that.

"I haven't thought much of marriage," he lied, standing and rocking back and forth from his toes to his heels as the uneasy thought grew within him at Eliza's eagerness to become intimate and now her discussion of marriage. "Perhaps sometime in the next few years."

"A few years," she repeated, her expression unchanged. "Well, I am tired. I think I shall retire for the night. I shall see you tomorrow?"

"Of course," he said, grateful that she had provided him with an escape. "Goodnight, Eliza." He leaned over and kissed her on the cheek before practically running from the room, stopping only to say, "Lock the door!" before running away down the hall.

CHAPTER 13

*E*liza couldn't shake the feeling that Fitz hadn't told her the entire truth about his plans for the future.

She had been so set against any interactions with him that she had never considered him as a potential husband. But now that she understood he hadn't been ignoring her but had, in fact, thought the opposite about her, she wondered why they wouldn't make a suitable pairing.

They got along well, they both shared a sense of adventure, and they were certainly compatible when it came to intimacy.

She would have to explore it further, but she wasn't the type of woman to trap a man into marriage. She could admit she was hurt by his outright rejection of the idea, but she would marry him only if he expressed any interest in it.

She was unsure what this was going to mean for the little experiment of theirs, but there were a few things that she would still like to try if he was up for it. She would have to make it clear that she had no expectations.

By the time she came downstairs to the breakfast room the following morning, the visitors were already having one more set of meetings before departing, according to Lady Fitzroy as they sat down to breakfast.

"I do hope the gentlemen leave shortly," Lady Fitzroy said, biting her bottom lip as she cast a look toward the door.

"Why?" Eliza's mother asked. "They seem polite enough, and I wouldn't mind Eliza spending more time with Lord Brighton."

"Mother, I have no interest in Lord Brighton," Eliza said, rolling her eyes as she lifted her teacup to her lips.

Before her mother could respond to that, Lady Fitzroy began speaking once more. "Because the girls are due home today."

"Are they?" Eliza said brightly, even as she wondered in the back of her mind if she would still have the opportunity to spend any time with Fitz.

"They are. They sent word just yesterday, but I didn't want to disturb Fitz with the news," she said. "I do know that he had no wish to have them here with three unwed men at the house."

"It would only be for the day," Eliza said, waving a hand in the air, certain that Fitz was just being dramatic, as usual. "I'm sure all would be fine."

"Be that as it may, I thought it best to keep it to myself," she said with a sigh. "Ah, here they are."

Eliza turned to see just who 'they' were, discovering it was the gentlemen, who were now dressed for travel.

"We have come to say farewell," Lord Brighton said with a smile, even though dark circles hung beneath his eyes in stark contrast to his pale skin. He had suffered from the self-affliction of too much drink. "Thank you for your hospitality." He stepped into the room toward Eliza, lifting her hand once more, this time his lips touching the bare skin of her hand. She shivered at the touch, but not because she was affected – more because his rough lips caused aversion within her.

Curious, for Fitz's had only caused fire.

She looked up, catching Fitz's eyes upon them. He was not happy. Not at all.

"Fitz!" A cry came from beyond the room, and Fitz's expression rapidly changed, from first a huge grin of happiness to a look of chagrin as his eyes flicked to the three gentlemen standing with him.

"I had no idea you would be home so soon," he said, leaving the men standing at the side of the breakfast room as he went to greet his sisters, Eliza quickly following suit. "It is good to see you."

"And you," Dot said, squeezing him as Henrietta spotted Eliza. "Eliza, what are you doing here?" she said, running toward her. Everyone made pleasantries, introducing those who did not know one another, and Eliza watched with interest as Lord Mandrake stared at Dot with perverse longing in his gaze.

Dot looked away, but a blush stole up her cheeks.

"Well, best get you men on the road before my sisters become overly chatty," Fitz said, trying to usher them away, but Lord Mandrake stopped, placing his hand on Dot's arm.

"Lady Dot, we never had that conversation," he began, but Fitz was there in moments.

"I already said no," he stated flatly. "Come, Mandrake, time to go."

"Fitz," Dot said, tilting her head, obviously not pleased with his reaction. "One conversation will not cause harm."

"Fine," he said tersely. "A conversation. Where I can see you."

Dot rolled her eyes at him before allowing Lord Mandrake to lead her beyond the room. Henrietta and Eliza exchanged a glance of interest before watching the two of them chat away. Eliza had no idea how two people who barely spoke would have so much to say, but Lord Mandrake must be more interesting than she would have thought.

She could practically feel Fitz bristling beside her, but

soon enough, Mandrake said his farewells and the gentlemen were thundering down the drive.

"You know, for a household that is supposed to be in hiding, you certainly have a lot of comings and goings," Eliza couldn't help but remark once the men were away.

"Too many, likely," Fitz said from behind her. "But the country's business cannot pause because of one little threat to one of its members. And my sisters cannot hide forever."

"Is there any word from the detective in London?" Sloane asked with a yawn.

"He did write to update me, but he hasn't found anything yet," Fitz said with a sigh. "I still think I should have stayed and tried to draw the person out."

"We should be safe," his mother said, placing a hand on his arm. "Now, ladies, it is a beautiful day. Why do we not spend it outside? We can have tea out there this afternoon and play a few games."

"A lovely idea," Lady Willoughby said, and Eliza exchanged a smile with Henrietta, who came over and squeezed her arm as they walked out of the room and upstairs to change.

"I am so glad you are here!" Henrietta said. "I apologize we were away. Had we known that you were coming, we never would have left."

"Of course!" Eliza said. "We should have written far sooner. How was Lady Noonan's?"

"As Mother told us it would be – boring!" she said with a laugh, as they headed up to their rooms to find their clothing for the outdoors.

As for Fitz? Well, she would have to worry about him later.

For there was nothing to do now but enjoy herself.

* * *

FITZ WAS BECOMING RATHER annoyed with his sisters.

Every time he tried to find a moment alone with Eliza, there they were, at her side. Even after they all retired for the night, he tried to go to her room, but when he was about to knock on her door, he saw the note attached to the doorknob warning him that Henrietta had decided to stay with her for the night.

He nearly pounded on the door in frustration.

She had become like a drug. He was addicted.

He barely saw her the next day besides at meal times, and it took everything within him not to spend the entire dinner staring at her, for he was well aware that his sisters would catch on to him if he did so.

Perhaps it was for the best. He had already compromised one young woman and look how that had nearly ended. He had almost been duped into a lifetime with a liar. Not that he could ever see Eliza doing such a thing, but he could not allow for any scandal to enter into his life.

He was more captivated by Eliza than he ever had been by any other woman. It was disconcerting, but he told himself it was only because the secrecy of all this had created an unmatched lust within him.

He couldn't help but ruminate on her words about marriage. Could he see himself married – and to her? He had a hard time picturing it. He was supposed to be finding a woman who would bring him respectability so that all would take him seriously. When the gentlemen had arrived from London, he had to fight with all of his powers of persuasion to get them even to consider backing his proposal.

Of course, Mandrake's accompaniment hadn't helped. The man had only traveled all of this way to try to put a hold on his plans, but Fitz would not be deterred.

Finally, two nights after they had come together, he was able to sneak into Eliza's bedroom without anyone spoiling his intentions.

"Fitz!" she said brightly, sitting up in bed. "I was wondering if I would ever see you again."

He loved her teasing laugh and he had to stop himself from bounding over to her.

"My sisters have monopolized you."

"So, you are interested in spending more time with me?" she said, raising her brows. "I thought perhaps it was all just talk the other night."

"Not talk," he said, shaking his head. "I meant what I said." He paused. "Although, I will not put you in any jeopardy again. I think it's time that we take a step backward."

"What does that mean?" she asked, closing her book and placing it on the nightstand beside her as the light in her eyes dimmed.

"That means," he said, curling his lips up as that mischievousness he had been trying to shed made itself known once more, "that we need to go back to lessons four and five. The ones we missed."

She bit her lip, obviously as affected as he was. "But I so enjoyed lesson six."

"It was enjoyable, yes," he said, nodding as though he was deep in thought. "But order is important, do you not agree?"

"No," she said laughing. "Do you not know me? That being said, I am a willing student, so I will obey my instructor."

"Obey you will," he said with a growl before practically diving on top of her, his lips landing on hers.

It seemed so much more proper this time, to be in a bed, and yet, proper was not exactly a term to describe anything related to Eliza. For she did not lie there and wait for him to take all of the initiative. She was just as eager as he was, wriggling beneath his grasp, responsive to his every touch, undressing him with the same urgency he did her.

When they were both naked to one another, he had to stop and compose himself, for he was worried that he was about to come right there in front of her before they had even touched one another.

"Fitz," she moaned as she ran her hands over him, her touch igniting his skin as though he had been burned, bucking her hips up into him. "Can we just—"

"No," he said, but he knew what she wanted even if she didn't herself. He ran his hands over those silky thighs that he couldn't get enough of before kneeling before her, lowering his face to her center.

She gasped as his tongue flicked against her, finding the bundle of nerves he knew would send her spiraling. She ground into him as he used his tongue, teeth, lips, and fingers to keep her on edge, never quite knowing what to expect from him.

"Fitz," she gasped again, his name coming on the edge of one of her pants.

"Yes?"

"I like lesson four."

He grinned wolfishly. "We're just getting started," he said before continuing his efforts. She had wanted to experience pleasure? Well, she would never experience anything like this ever again. He would be unmatched. Of that, he would make sure.

CHAPTER 14

Eliza was still coming down from the high Fitz had taken her to as they lay on her bed and she stared dreamily at the ceiling, her eyes lazily following the intricate gold-leaf flower and vine motifs that covered the wooden beams.

"Tell me something about you," she said dreamily.

"Like what?"

"Anything. Something no one else knows."

Fitz paused, rubbing a hand over his forehead as he seemed to consider her question. "How about my name?"

"Your name?"

"My Christian name," he said, flipping over onto his stomach to stare at her, a large grin widening over his face. "Do you know it?"

She bit her lip. She must know it. How could she not? But the more she considered it, the more she realized that he was right – she had no idea what his name was.

"Very well," she said. "You are right. I don't know it."

"Christian."

"Yes, you said that. Your Christian name."

"No." He laughed, and she couldn't help noting with a

sigh just how handsome he was. "That's my name. Christian."

"Truly?" She had no idea why she found that so hard to believe. "You do not look like a Christian."

He laughed even louder. "I know. That's why everyone calls me Fitz – even my mother. I know it is not custom to be called by one's title while one's father is alive, but, when I was a young boy, my father said that I looked nothing like a Christian. He began to call me 'young Fitz,' and soon enough the name shortened and stuck. So, Fitz I am."

"It's perfect for you," Eliza said, her voice softening as she appreciated that he would share such a story with her. "Your father sounds like he was a wonderful man."

"He was," Fitz said ruefully. "I wish I'd had more time with him."

"How old were you when he passed?"

"Twenty. It was sudden. I was... otherwise occupied when I should have been learning from him."

Eliza nodded, caught between wanting to know more about Fitz and his emotions and wondering if she should try to bring back the jovial Fitz. She sensed, however, that he needed to speak about this. Perhaps he never had before.

"That would have been hard for your mother and your sisters," she said. She hadn't known his family well then and couldn't remember what the previous Lord Fitzroy had been like.

"It was," he said, his lips firming into a line. "I should have been there for them."

"I'm sure you did all you could."

"I didn't," he said, his voice fierce and dripping with self-doubt. "I was caught up in something else entirely. Something I had no business being involved in."

"Do you wish to speak of it?" she asked, hesitant, for she wondered if she was going to like what he had to say.

"It had to do with a woman," he finally said, no longer

meeting her eyes. "A woman who was nothing more than a liar, who wanted to use me for my title."

"I see," she said quietly, longing to know more but also not wanting to seem desperate to know that part of him. It wasn't her business, after all, not if he only wanted to spend time with her in bed and nowhere else. "You are making up for it now, Fitz. You're a good brother. Trust me. I know how much your sisters love you."

"That's good to know, even if I don't deserve it," he said before falling silent.

Eliza waited for him to say more, but when he didn't, she decided to try another tactic. She trailed her fingers down his body, beginning at his collarbone and slowly inching her way down, over the springy hairs of his chest to the muscles of his abdomen, until they finally played with the edge of his breeches.

"What are you doing?" he asked, his voice thick.

"I think I'm ready for lesson five."

"We don't have to."

"I want to," she said, biting her bottom lip. "If you feel up to it."

He let out a snort that she knew was him coming back to her and the present moment. "I can't imagine a time I wouldn't be."

He wrapped his arms around her back, flipping them over so that he was lying on the bed with her on top of him. He unfastened the fall of his breeches, shimmying them down his legs, until Eliza grabbed them and threw them to the floor beside them. Her eyes went wide as she stared at him, wondering how he had possibly fit inside of her, before she went to her knees before him, her hands bracketing his legs.

"Use your hands if you'd like," he suggested, but she shook her head. She had seen this in the book and had always been curious about it. Now that she had experienced what Fitz had offered her, she was ready to do the same for him.

She did wrap one of her hands around the bottom of his member, but then slowly lowered her head until she was hovering right over top of him. She grinned to herself before she leaned down, taking just the tip of him in her mouth. He groaned as he arched his back in supplication toward her, and finally, she took pity on him, leaning down and taking him fully in her mouth.

Not entirely sure what she was doing, Eliza decided that her best option was to experiment. Recalling how Fitz had played with her, she used her lips, her tongue, and her hand to fully explore him and stroke him, paying attention to what caused the greatest reaction from him and resolving to do more of it.

She began to stroke the underside of his cock with her tongue as she used her hand to squeeze him up and down as she had in the past, and he cried out her name as he began to pulse beneath her.

"Eliza," he said. "You can come off now. I'm—"

But Eliza remembered what the book had said and resolved to stay with him. She shuddered slightly at the shock of the sensation when he came inside her mouth, but she kept her mouth around him, taking all of him in, and he quickly provided her with a handkerchief to clean up.

"Are you all right?" he said quietly. "I'm sorry, I—"

"Did you like that?" she asked eagerly, and his eyes widened.

"Like it?" he repeated. "I loved it."

"Good," she said, practically bouncing toward him and throwing her arms around him. "I'm so glad."

They fell to the bed together, wrapped in each other's embrace. It was warm and comforting, and Eliza stilled, wondering if she liked this far too much. But his body was heavy around her, and she found that instead of backing away, it felt much better to burrow into him. Soon her eyes grew heavy and while she knew she should say goodnight and suggest he leave her room, she figured she could relax with him for just a few moments longer.

The next thing she knew, it was morning and he was gone.

What bothered her the most was how much she already missed him.

* * *

THE NEXT FEW weeks passed by quickly.

Between spending time with Henrietta, Sloane, Dot, and the rest of Fitz's sisters during the day and sneaking into Fitz's room or he to hers through the night, Eliza was enjoying herself more than she had in quite some time. She missed Siena, whom she had grown used to seeing nearly every day for the past few years, but she knew that she was going to have to become accustomed to being without her. Siena was married now, and soon enough would have a family of her own.

The thought of her closest friend in the world not having time for her caused sadness in her heart, but there was nothing to be done about it. It was how the world worked.

Eliza had a much more significant – and pressing problem, anyway. One she wasn't aware of until dinner that evening.

"Fitz, have you heard from the detective in London?" Lady Fitzroy asked.

"I've heard from him, but nothing promising," Fitz said, laying his fork down as he looked over the rest of them. "As I am no longer in London, there doesn't seem to be much to investigate. As for the previous attempts on my life, the trail to the source has grown cold. Whoever planned this was careful — if this was even a true plan."

"What does that mean?" Dot asked, her nose crinkling.

"Maybe I overreacted. Maybe there was nothing to run away from," he said. "What if it was just a coincidence that the two events occurred? What if I was mistaken for another?

I am just another lord. Who would have anything to gain by being rid of me?"

"It's not worth taking the risk," his mother said firmly.

"It's been over four weeks since we left London," he said, splaying his hands out in front of him. "How long are we to wait here in the country for nothing to happen?"

The conversation continued around the table, but Eliza suddenly found that it all became background noise.

Four weeks.

Four weeks since Fitz's family had been in the countryside. She and her mother had arrived a week later, and she had Fitz had come together just a few days after that. She hadn't had her monthly courses since she had been in London. About a week before she had left, if she remembered correctly, for she recalled her mother wanting her to accompany her to the Rutherfords' ball and she had declined for she had been feeling rather poorly.

She was so regular, they should have started at least a week ago.

Oh no.

Heat rushed into her cheeks as she began to fan her face, the overwhelm suddenly washing over her.

"Eliza? Eliza are you all right?" Her mother's voice broke through her thoughts as Eliza hurriedly pushed back her chair.

"Excuse me a moment," she said and, ignoring all of the shocked stares that followed her, she rushed out the door blindly. She didn't know where she was going.

She just knew she had to get away.

CHAPTER 15

Fitz had to fight everything within him to prevent himself from running after Eliza. How would it look to his family if he was the one who took off after her to ensure that she was well?

She had appeared ill so suddenly. One moment she was laughing and joking with the rest of them, the next, she seemed about to run from the room as though she had been punched in the stomach.

What had they been talking about? He tried to recall the conversation as Eliza's mother went after her to ensure that she was well. The threat to his life. Was that what had caused her reaction? Was she so worried about him that it had made her sick? That didn't seem to be in character for her. For one, he wasn't certain that she cared that much about him, and for another, she usually contained her emotions.

Fortunately, they were nearly finished dinner and they decided that with Eliza and her mother no longer accompanying them, they would retire early that night.

Fitz was practically pacing around his study as he waited until a suitable hour to go to Eliza, not wanting to encounter her mother or her maid along the way.

As it happened, he didn't have long to wait, for before he could even leave his study, the door was opening, and Eliza was slipping through.

She was already dressed for bed in her nightgown and wrapper, and Fitz tamped down his surge of desire, reminding himself that she was not feeling well, which meant that he shouldn't expect anything, nor ask for it unless it was her idea.

"Eliza," he said, hurriedly crossing toward her, gripping her upper arms in his hands before running them over her as though checking for injury. "Are you well? I've been worried."

"Worried about me, are you?" she said in what he assumed was supposed to be a teasing tone, but he could see the concern in her eyes and couldn't stop his questions.

"What is it?" he asked. "What's happened? Was it something I said?"

She pulled her hands away from him, wringing them in front of her as she began to slowly pace back and forth across the room, her gaze on the floor. For the first time, Fitz was scared, his heart beating so strongly that he wondered if she could hear it.

"It was something you said, actually," she said, and his heart flopped over in his chest at the thought that he had hurt her, even if it had been unintentional. "But only because it reminded me of something," she continued.

"Something from your past?"

"From the past… and the future," she said cryptically.

"What is that supposed to mean?"

She took a deep breath before stopping her movements back and forth and staring at him, her hands folded in front of her, her feet in a firm stance beneath her, even as he couldn't help his continued back-and-forth rocking.

"You said you had been here for four weeks."

"Yes. Far too long," he said gruffly, knowing that if Eliza

hadn't been with him, he might have gone mad with all of the time he would have been alone.

"Which means it has been three weeks since I left London."

"Yes," he said, not following.

"We began our little experiment a few days after I arrived, and the last time that I… that I had my… monthly womanly time was two weeks before that."

A sick feeling of dread sprung up in his stomach as he knew far too well what she was saying, even as he wanted to deny the truth.

"Are you saying you are with child?" he whispered, although the words seemed to be coming from far away, from someone else entirely.

"I don't know," she said, her voice equally soft and low as well. "Maybe?"

"Yes or no?" he demanded, knowing that he was being brutish but unable to help it as past experiences began to wash over him. He had been down this path before and had no wish to walk it again.

"I suppose yes unless anything changes in the next few days," she said, her voice still hushed as her eyes widened in fear.

"Is it mine?" he found himself saying, the words forming on his tongue.

"What?" she said, her eyes snapping up to his, fire replacing the fear.

"I said, is it mine? Don't lie to me," he said, his hands in fists at his side as he was nearly shaking before her.

"What is that supposed to mean?" she said, her anger forming. "Of course it is, you blockhead! Who else's would it be?"

He shrugged. "Anyone's. You said you came here to learn. To experiment. Well, you seemed pretty well-informed already. Maybe this was your plan. You knew that you were with child, so you came here to convince me that it was mine. That's why you brought up marriage, wasn't it? Planting the seeds just like you had me believe I was planting mine in you?"

He could see his words were hurting her, but he couldn't help them as they spewed forth. His hurt and anger had overwhelmed him, washing away any rational thought or empathy.

He had wondered how her feelings toward him had changed so suddenly from hatred to familiarity, and it was all beginning to make sense. Why she had wanted to be intimate with him so quickly, how she had no qualms about making love to him and had ensured that he finished inside of her, even when he knew he should have done otherwise.

"Fitz," she said, anguish in her voice once she finally formed the word. "How could you say such things? I would never—you know me better than that."

"Do I?" he said. "How well do I really know you?"

"I thought better than this," she said, her nostrils flaring. "I will tell you one thing. I hope I am wrong. I hope I am only late because, after this, I would prefer to have nothing more to do with you. I have no wish to be with a man who thinks so ill of me, and I would rather never see you again."

He sighed, raking a hand through his hair as reason and past experiences warred within him. "It just all seems rather convenient, Eliza. You must realize that, do you not?"

"It takes two people to come together, Fitz," she said, beginning to blink rapidly, and he realized with great chagrin that she was near tears. Damn, but he hated when his sisters cried. He didn't want to think about Eliza doing so, especially when it was because of him. "I don't know what it is you have against me, but I shall figure this out on my own. I thought you would want to know, that this was *our* problem, and you would support me. That is why I came to you. So we could determine a way forward together. But now... now I see that this has all been a great mistake."

Before he could say anything further, she had flung open the door and was running down the hallway. He rushed to the threshold and looked out, seeing only the material of her wrapper flying behind her, her bare feet slapping against the hardwood floor, softening when she reached the runner covering the stairs.

She nearly stumbled on the first step, catching herself on the railing just in time, and Fitz hesitated in the doorway, caught between running after her and staying exactly where he was.

Which, he realized, was the problem. He was stuck between the past and the present.

He pressed his lips together. If he hadn't learned from his previous mistakes, then what was the point of it all? He wouldn't be trapped again. Of that, he was certain.

* * *

ELIZA FLUNG herself down on her bed as the pit of unease that had sprung up during dinner only grew bigger.

Please let this just be poor timing, she prayed. She hoped that she was not with child, for if she was, she had very few options. Her mother was understanding of most things in her life, but this would most certainly cross the line. Her parents would insist that she tell them who the father was and would then make sure that they were married. Anything else would be a complete scandal for herself, her family, and her unborn child.

The worst part of it all was that there was no reason she could see why she and Fitz *couldn't* be married.

No reason, that was, until he had opened his mouth and responded to her tonight. She knew that he had been hurt in his past, that much was obvious, but if he truly thought her such an awful woman, then why had he spent any time with her in the first place?

She supposed that, if anything, this proved that she didn't know him as well as she had thought, either. For the Fitz she thought she knew would never treat her like he had just done. She should have stayed away in the first place.

One thing was certain. She was in a pickle. She could only hope that it would be solved in the next two days, or she was in a heap of trouble.

Even more than she currently was.

And that was saying something.

CHAPTER 16

Eliza stayed in bed for the entire next day.

She told her mother she was still feeling the ill effects from whatever had overcome her the night before, a fact which was not a lie.

She wasn't sure if it was the recognition of the situation, the potential that she was actually with child, or how Fitz had reacted to everything, but it felt like there was a ball in the pit of her stomach that had become painful. She felt best lying in bed with her knees tucked beneath her. While she knew that she couldn't spend forever in this chamber, for today, it was where she had to stay.

Then her maid walked in with a tray of ham, eggs, and rolls, and Eliza gagged, nearly becoming sick.

Her maid quickly hurried out, and it wasn't long until Henrietta and Sloane arrived in her stead.

"Eliza?" Sloane said with some hesitation. "Are you well?"

"Not really," she said, wishing she could speak of this, but she most certainly could not tell Fitz's sisters anything about her precarious predicament.

There was only one person she could speak to about this.

Siena. Eliza wondered if her letter had made it to Siena through the post. She closed her eyes as she thought back to the joy with which she had written it despite her confusion, and how much her situation had changed from that day to now.

"I must ask a favor of you," she said. "Has any mail arrived for me?"

"Not that I know of, but I can ask Hastings," Henrietta said with a kind smile. "Is there anything else we can do for you?"

"No," Eliza said, covering her mouth with her hand before the moan could escape. "Thank you."

"Of course," Henrietta said, patting the bed beside her before she and Sloane left the room.

Eliza must have slept for a few hours, for when she woke to a knock sounding on the door, the sunlight was no longer shining through the window. Remnants of tears sat upon her eyelashes. She assumed her mother was at the door, and she had to blink a few times for her figure to come into focus.

"Oh, I am so sorry, I didn't mean to wake you," came the soft, familiar, and oh, so incredibly welcome voice.

"Siena!" Eliza cried out, practically flinging herself out of bed toward her friend, pausing to assess how she felt, relieved to find that her symptoms seemed to have abated. She patted Siena up and down her arms to convince herself that she was actually present. "What are you doing here?"

"I received your letter and could read what you were not telling me – that you needed someone to speak to. I can imagine it would be rather difficult to explain all of this to Henrietta and Sloane, even now that they have returned."

"Yes, it most certainly would be," Eliza said, taking Siena's hand and leading her over to the bed. "Is the duke here as well?"

"He is," Siena said, a soft smile gracing her lips, and Eliza's heart jumped in happiness that her friend had found such a love. "He would never want me to travel this far alone. Besides, I think he misses Fitz, even if he won't admit it."

Eliza leaned in. "How much did you tell him about my letter?" she asked in a whisper.

"Not much," Siena said, shaking her head. "Just that you and Fitz had become close. He was surprised, for the two of you barely spoke when you were at Greystone."

"That was by design, apparently," Eliza said, biting her lip before telling Siena what Fitz had said about being attracted to her and forcing himself to avoid her.

"Well, that is interesting," Siena said, looking around as though she had a secret even though they were alone in the bedroom before dropping her voice down low. "How were your… relations? Were they everything you had imagined?"

"Oh, Siena," Eliza said with a large sigh and a chuckle. "They were so much more."

They giggled for a moment before Eliza sobered, holding Siena's hands in hers. "There is, however, a problem. A great problem."

Siena waited patiently for Eliza to continue.

"I believe I might be with child," Eliza said, her voice so low that Siena had to lean in to hear her. Goodness, why could she not speak louder when discussing this? It was almost as though she believed that if she kept it quiet enough, it wouldn't be true, but of course, her belief wouldn't cause any change.

Siena's eyes widened, her mouth forming a round O.

"Oh, Eliza," she said, gripping her hands within hers even tighter. "Oh, dear."

She sat like that for so long that Eliza tilted her head to study her. "Siena?"

"I'm so sorry," she said, shaking her head. "I am just shocked, is all. I suppose I shouldn't be. It is a natural result."

She bit her lip, looking up at Eliza. "Does it help that I am as well?"

"Siena!" Eliza said, bouncing her bottom up and down on the bed excitedly. "Congratulations." Siena's greatest wish had always been to be a mother, so it truly was the most wonderful news.

"Thank you," Siena said, squeezing Eliza's hands. "But I do not want to overshadow – nor ignore – your situation."

"My situation," Eliza said with a sigh, shaking her head. "Yes. I do hope that my cycle is simply late, however I am always so regularly on time that it seems far too great a coincidence that it would be late the one time that I have been with a man."

"Have you told Fitz?"

"Yes," Eliza said, her tone harsher than she intended before she recounted their conversation – if one could call it that – from the night before.

"He truly said that?" Siena said, aghast.

"Yes."

"I can hardly believe it," Siena said, crossing her arms over her chest. "I can understand his shock, but he is just as much a part of this as you are. Besides, what would be so terrible as the two of you being married?"

"I wish I knew," Eliza returned. "But it seems that it is not something he wishes to even consider. I could understand his reluctance, but his accusations were another insult entirely. I believe he thinks that I am trying to trap him into marriage, but I can assure you that I would have no desire to marry a man who had no wish to be with me nor thinks so ill of me."

"Of course," Siena murmured before shaking her head. "He will come around. I am sure of it. Men can be rather obstinate sometimes."

"Sometimes?" Eliza snorted. "All the time."

"Do you wish to go for a walk?" Siena asked suddenly, rising from the bed.

"A walk?"

"I find that fresh air clears both my head and stomach,"

Siena said with a small smile. "If you are truly with child, then it will be some time before you are feeling any better."

Eliza groaned and threw herself back on the bed as Siena laughed and crossed over to Eliza's wardrobe to find her a gown that she could wear outdoors.

The only way Eliza's situation could improve was for this all to come to naught – but at least Siena was here.

She was sure she could get through this.

She just had to figure out how.

* * *

FITZ HADN'T BEEN able to stay in the same house as Eliza for another moment. He didn't even wait to see if she was coming for breakfast that morning. Instead, he had gone for a ride to clear his head so that he could see through to the truth of the matter and determine just what he was supposed to do.

A child. Someday, he would likely be a father, but he had never taken the time to consider just what that would actually mean. And with Eliza. She was such a bright light, but was she *too* bright?

He closed his eyes as he tried to imagine a life with her. It would be fun, that was for certain. But he could only imagine the talk if he disappeared from London and returned with a wife and child on the way just a few months later. No one would take him seriously. But what other choice did he have?

Fitz reached the long, open field where he liked to allow the horse to have his fill stretching his legs when he noted motion beside him. He turned quickly, prepared to defend himself, but instead, a wide grin stretched across his face and the tension within him eased when he saw who was there.

"Levi!"

He pulled up on his horse as his friend did the same. "What are you doing here?"

He was so relieved that when he dismounted, he nearly

wrapped his friend in a hug, but of course, that would never do between the two of them.

"My wife told me she needed to come to see Eliza," Levi said, never one to waste any words.

"So, you came as well?"

"I have no wish to leave her side anytime soon."

"Of course," Fitz said, recalling all Levi and his wife had been through. He could understand Levi's wish to stay close to ensure that Siena remained safe. "And you wanted to see me, of course."

Levi snorted and shook his head, but Fitz saw the spark in his eye that told him he wasn't far off the mark. He and Levi had been friends for ages, as much as Levi always refused to acknowledge what they meant to one another. No matter. Fitz was always there to remind him.

"I hear you've been in some danger," Levi said as they began to walk their horses side by side.

"Potentially," Fitz said before relaying the story. "I am beginning to believe that it was all in my imagination."

"Will you return to London to see if anything comes of it?"

"I have been contemplating it," Fitz said, knowing that he likely would have done so far sooner had it not been for Eliza. "I cannot hide here forever. I would ask my mother and sisters to stay in the country until I have an answer one way or another. I do not suppose that would go over well, but I'm not sure what else I am supposed to do."

He looked down at his hands and fisted them around the reins, wondering how much he should tell Levi, but then realized that Eliza would definitely not be holding any information back from Siena.

"There is another matter. One much more… sensitive."

He told Levi of all that had occurred with Eliza, including the news she had imparted the night before.

"You didn't realize that could happen?" Levi said, no

change in his expression, and Fitz would have stomped his foot on the ground if he hadn't been mounted.

"Of course I did! I just hoped... that it wouldn't. Besides," he said, shrugging his shoulders, "I am not certain that she actually is with child. Or that the baby is mine."

"Why would you say that?" Levi asked without judgment, and Fitz recounted his suspicions.

"Well," Levi responded, "it would certainly become apparent in due time as to whether or not she is lying about being with child. Although if you waited to marry her, it would be fairly late and quite obvious as to what brought about your wedded bliss."

Fitz nodded as Levi laid out all the arguments that he had been reviewing himself.

"As to whose baby it would be... I know that I cannot be certain, but from what Siena has told me about Eliza, I would have a hard time believing she was with another man and then contrived to trap you into this."

"But you cannot be sure."

"One can never be sure about anything."

"How do I know?"

"At some point, I suppose you have to decide whether or not you trust her."

Fitz shot him a hard look. "When did you become the voice of reason?"

Levi released a low chuckle. "I was always reasonable. I just decided to start sharing my thoughts since I have obviously made such wonderful choices myself."

Fitz snorted as Levi turned to look at him more closely.

"How much does this have to do with Jessica?"

"I do not like to speak about her."

"Of course you don't. But this situation is remarkably similar."

"Too similar," Fitz said, shaking his head as they turned

the horses back toward the house, although he wasn't ready to enter it yet and face Eliza or any of his family.

"You are biased because of it."

"How could I not be? Jessica did this very thing. She told me she was with child, and I nearly married her, until the father of her baby came to me and told me the truth of it all. That they were without means and had planned to use me to support the child."

"How did you know that he wasn't lying to you?" Levi asked, and Fitz pushed back the brim of his hat to meet his gaze.

"I felt it in my gut."

"And you were right – that baby came just six months after you had been together."

"Imagine if I had married her. What my life would be like."

"You would have made it work."

"Perhaps, but what life would that be, one built upon a foundation of lies – if she had even stayed?"

"Not a particularly pleasant one, I imagine," Levi said, and they rode in silence for a few moments.

"After I escaped the trap, I told myself that when I did marry, it would be a practical, advantageous match. Yet here I am again."

"What do you feel now? You said your gut reaction told you the truth before. What is it telling you now, about Eliza?"

Fitz closed his eyes, trusting his horse to know the way, before opening them and looking at Levi with clarity.

"She is not one to fabricate stories."

Levi said nothing, waiting for Fitz to come to the realization himself.

"She's telling the truth, isn't she?"

Levi only stared at him with his one good eye, the other hidden by the eye patch.

"Damn it," Fitz said, shaking his head as he stared ahead. "I guess I'm going to have to marry her."

CHAPTER 17

"Here they come."

Eliza turned, her gaze following to where Siena was pointing. Sure enough, Fitz and Levi were cresting the hill on their horses.

"What do you think they are talking about?" she asked Siena.

"The same thing we were, I imagine," Siena said. "Hopefully, Levi was able to talk some sense into him."

They were walking among the orchard outside of Appleton. The trees were blossoming, and Eliza knew that they would produce the most gorgeous fruit in nearly no time at all.

Almost like herself, she thought with a laugh.

"Perhaps if we hide, they won't see us," Eliza said wryly, but Siena only smiled and shook her head, gazing into the distance.

"Levi could find me, no matter where I hid."

Eliza couldn't help her smirk, but their love was rather adorable.

"At this point, I am not sure that I would want to marry Fitz, even if he asked," Eliza said, crossing her arms and turning away from the approaching men toward Siena, who lifted a brow.

"What is your alternate solution?"

"I suppose live with my parents, concoct some story about how I married a soldier who died in battle before the birth, and then raise the baby alone."

Siena blinked.

"You came up with that story rather quickly."

"What can I say? I'm a natural storyteller," she said with a wry grin before continuing. "There is one other option."

"Which is?"

"Do exactly what Fitz accused me of. Find another man to quickly court me, fall in love with me, marry me, and then pretend the baby came early. I would never be intimate with him until after our marriage to pretend it was so, but the rest I could probably do. Perhaps Lord Brighton would be interested. I know my mother approves."

Hope leaped into her heart that there could be a solution, and she turned around to hurry back to the house and suggest that it was time to return to London. Before she could take a step, however, she ran into something tall, hard, and very frowny.

"Fitz," she said, stepping backward, annoyed that he had been able to sneak up on her. "Why are you so close to me?"

"You will *not* marry Lord Brighton," he said, nostrils flaring as he crossed his arms over his chest.

"I'm sorry, but I don't think you have any say in the matter," she said, standing toe to toe with him, refusing to back down.

He pointed at her stomach. "As that is my baby, I most certainly do."

"Oh, you are claiming the baby now? I thought it was someone else's – if it even exists at all," she returned, her ire matching his.

"I believe Levi and I will go explore the orchard. We will

not be far," Eliza dimly heard Siena murmur, but she was too concentrated on her battle with Fitz to respond.

"Baby or not, you will not go to Lord Brighton. For courting or love or marriage or any of your damn experiments."

"Lord Brighton is only one option," she said, stepping to the side to go around him. "I might find someone else. I am sure many suitors would be interested in me."

He stepped with her, blocking her path. "You will not."

"Fitz," she said, unable to stop herself from reaching out and shoving at his chest, all of her pent-up frustrations coming through. "Get out of my way. I'm sorry, but in case you hadn't noticed, there are few other options available for a woman in my – likely – condition."

She pushed at him again, but this time he caught her wrists in his hands, holding them close to his chest.

"You will not marry any of them," he said firmly, looking into her eyes. "Because you will marry me instead."

He leaned down and, before she knew what was happening, pressed his lips against hers.

* * *

FITZ WASN'T sure what had come over him.

He had agreed to marry her, yes, but he wasn't exactly happy about it. Then, when they had walked up to the women in the orchard and he had overheard Eliza telling Siena of her plans, a possessive rage had come over him at the thought of her ever being with anyone else.

The words emerged before he even had a chance to consider them, and in that moment, he had been unable to prevent himself from capturing her lips, drinking her in, knowing deep within him that as much as he had told himself a union with her would be all wrong, this was right for him.

She kissed him back for a few moments, her passion for

him clear, until she suddenly broke the kiss, leaned back, and shoved him away.

She was surprisingly powerful for a woman of her size.

"What," she seethed, "do you think you are doing?"

"Kissing my bride," he said, puffing his chest out with the possession of his words.

"In case you hadn't noticed, I have not yet agreed," she retorted.

"You told me you wanted to be married!" he countered, throwing his hands up in the air.

"Yes, before you were a complete ass."

"I do not believe that is language a proper young lady should use."

"At what point in our relations did I ever strike you as a *proper young lady*?"

They were standing face to face, both of their chests heaving, and damn it, but he did want to kiss her again. Was it worth the risk? Probably. But reason prevailed and he did begin to slowly back away, as though if he moved too quickly, she might attack – or flee.

"Is that a yes?" he asked, lifting a brow, and she let out a growl and fisted her hands at her sides.

"No!"

"I thought this was what you wanted! When will you make a final decision?" he asked, flabbergasted. Eliza was changing her mind from one moment to the next faster than a weathervane in a storm.

"When I determine whether or not I am with child!" she yelled, forgetting herself.

And the fact that anyone could be walking through the orchard.

Which, as it happened, they were.

"Eliza Gertrudis Munroe, what did you just say?"

Eliza froze as still as a statue, her eyes wide, her lips parted.

Fitz whirled around, stilling himself when he saw their mothers standing there in a fair state of distress.

He knew his problems had increased exponentially, and yet, he couldn't stop himself from focusing on one thing he knew should not matter. And yet...

He looked at Eliza. "Did she just call you *Gertrudis*?"

Her lips parted as she stared at him incredulously. "What importance could that possibly hold right now?"

"A great deal of importance if you have any inkling of naming my child that."

Eliza placed her hands on her hips as she looked down her nose at him. "Do you seriously think I would name my child something so hideous?"

"Eliza!" her mother started, her hand flying to her breast.

"I'm sorry, Mother, I know it was the name of your favorite great-aunt, but while you were an obedient daughter and listened to your mother, I have not fallen suit. I am certainly not going to begin by naming my daughter such a monstrous name."

"I rather like the Gertrude part of it," Fitz's mother murmured beside Lady Willoughby, placing a comforting hand on her back before clearing her throat.

"Based on this conversation... do the two of you have news to share with us, perhaps of a *betrothal*?"

Fitz tried to meet Eliza's gaze but was unable to do so as she currently had her eyes closed, her head tilted up toward the sky in supplication, as though she was waiting for the heavens to open and save her from this situation.

This situation, meaning him and potentially, his child.

Lady Willoughby was currently fanning herself as though the heat of the day – or this conversation – had overcome her.

"We were just speaking about that, actually," he said with pleasantness as though he was referring to whether or not they were going to take tea together that afternoon.

"This is all my fault," Lady Willoughby was murmuring,

wringing her hands together as she stared into the distance. "I was far too lenient. I thought I was doing the right thing to let her do as she wanted but now… oh dear… I was wrong."

"Mother!" Eliza exclaimed, her mother's reaction snapping her out of her own. "Do not say that, please," she said as she rushed over and took her mother's hands. "You are the best *woman* I have ever known, let alone the best mother. You have done nothing wrong, I promise you that."

"Yes, but…" her mother started, bringing a hand to her forehead as she gestured toward Fitz and then Eliza's middle region with her other. "This should not have happened."

"Perhaps not," Eliza agreed. "But all is not lost."

"You are unmarried," her mother bit out. "With child."

"I believe I am with child, yes," Eliza agreed, looking over at Fitz. Her expression was not the one of resignation he expected but rather one that said, well, they were now in this together. "I am unmarried at the moment, but that will not be an issue for much longer."

"You'll marry me, then?" Fitz said, surprised at the excitement in his tone. Excitement that was coming from an unexpected place within him.

He still couldn't say that he completely trusted Eliza, although he had been telling the truth when he told Levi that his instinct said she would never contrive such a thing.

If he was doing this, however – and now, it seemed that he had no choice – then he was all in, as he was in whatever he did.

Wife, child, family – it was coming hurtling toward him at a frightening speed. And yet he was going to welcome it.

He didn't have much other choice.

"Yes," she said with a nod, her eyes fiery as she stared at him. "I will marry you."

CHAPTER 18

Eliza's future might be out of her hands now, but she was not a woman to sit around and allow things to happen to her. She needed answers – and there was only one man who could provide them.

Which was why she was now sitting in his bedchamber awaiting his arrival, tapping her foot impatiently, even though he did not know that she was here.

After the confrontation between Eliza, Fitz, and their mothers in the orchard, the women had convened in the drawing room. Even though all of the ladies who were closest to her in the entire world had been at her side – her mother, Siena, Henrietta, Sloane, as well as the rest of the women in Fitz's family – Eliza's cheeks had remained rather heated as she had stumbled through a half-fabricated explanation about how she and Fitz had drawn closer over the past few weeks and had decided that they would be well matched.

Eliza had seen the rather skeptical expressions on the women's faces, but they had accepted the story – what other choice did they have?

She sat up quickly now in the armchair in front of the fireplace when the door opened, and Fitz stepped into the room.

He didn't immediately look up, as he was rubbing his fists over his eyes, giving her the opportunity to take a closer look at him without him noticing.

She had always found him striking. Add that to his charm and it was easy to see why women were so intrigued by him.

She wondered if that was going to be a problem in their marriage. If theirs would even be a marriage in truth or one in name like she had heard of so many times before. How sad would that be?

His hands fluttered away from his face, which was full of exhaustion. Was that all because of her or were there other factors at play?

"Fitz?" she said tentatively, and he jumped when he saw her.

"Eliza," he said, bringing his hand to his chest. "What are you doing here?"

His eyes instantly lit up as they ran over her body in interest, but that wasn't her intention.

"I am here to talk to you." She paused, looking at him meaningfully. "And only to talk."

"Very well," he said cautiously. "What would you like to talk about?"

"About why you reacted to me the way you did," she said, blinking away the tears beginning to form in her eyes as she recalled how his words had hurt her. "What did you want me to do, Fitz? Not tell you? And the fact that you assumed such awful things about me—"

Her voice broke, and she dipped her head downward, not wanting him to see how he had affected her.

"Eliza," he said gruffly, and when she looked up, his hands were in his pockets as he scuffed his toe against the floor. "I'm sorry."

"You're sorry?" she scoffed, annoyed that he thought two simple words could fix the hateful ones he had spewed earlier. "Very well, but I'm going to need a little more of an explanation than that. You may think that we do not know one another well, but I thought you had become well enough acquainted with me to know that I would never try to trap you into anything. We had agreed on an experiment, but we did spend a good amount of time together and I thought we were... friends, if nothing else. Until your reaction to my news."

He rubbed his temples as he took the matching chair across from her, slouching down within it, his elbows coming to his knees.

"You're right," he practically mumbled, and she had to lean in to properly hear him. "It wasn't just about you."

"Then what was it?"

"I'd rather not speak of it."

"Just as I would rather not be in this predicament with you, but here we are."

He sighed as he tilted his head back, looking up at the ceiling before finally dropping his chin.

"Very well," he said, waiting a beat before continuing. "I was in another... situation before."

She lifted her brows. "Are you referring to the woman you said you thought you would build a life with?"

"That's the one," he said. "She also told me that she was with child and that the child was mine. She was the widow of a minor lord, so someone who I thought I could just... have some fun with." He cringed. "I realize how that sounds."

"Oh, do go on," she said, annoyed, but mostly with herself for how she was reacting to his story of another woman.

"I agreed to marry her, even though she was not the woman I would have wanted to marry nor was I ready to marry at the time. However, I knew if I didn't do the right thing, there would be scandal."

Eliza could see where this story was going. "Was she lying about being with child?"

"No, on that she was telling the truth. Only, it wasn't my child."

Well, that was interesting.

"Did she lie on purpose?"

"She did," he said, nodding grimly. "Along with her lover who was the father of the baby. They concocted some scheme to have me believe the baby was mine. The plan was that by the time we were married and I realized the timing of the pregnancy, it would be too late for me to deny anything."

"How did you learn the truth?" Eliza asked, more invested in this story than she liked.

"The father came to me and told me what they had done. He said that his conscience made him confess, but I am fairly certain that the impetus was his jealousy that she was with another man and that I would be raising his child as my own."

Eliza absorbed his story, trying to make sense of it and everything that had followed between her and Fitz.

"I can see the similarities, of course, and can better understand your reaction," she said. "I still wish you hadn't assumed I was just like this woman."

"I know," he said, his head still facing the carpet. "I can see that now. I do trust that you are telling me the truth. It just… shocked me for a moment. Took me back to another time."

As much as she would like to hold onto her annoyance at how he had treated her, she couldn't change the past – she could only make certain that it wouldn't happen again.

"I would appreciate it if we could start anew," she said. "Why do we not do all of this over?"

"Do what over?"

"I'm telling you the news," she said. He eyed her with uncertainty but eventually nodded.

"Very well."

She closed her eyes, inhaling deeply as she assumed character.

"Fitz?"

"Yes, Eliza?"

"I have reason to believe that I am with child."

His expression flickered for a moment as though he was uncertain whether to continue with this charade. Eventually, he gave in to it.

"My goodness, Eliza, that is some surprising news." He was fairly good at this. Were he not an earl, he could have had a career on the stage.

"I can understand that this might come as a shock."

"It certainly does."

"It did to me as well. That's why I was so overcome when I realized the truth of it."

"I… assume that I am the only man you have ever had relations with."

"You assume correctly," she said, giving him a hard look.

"Well…" He cleared his throat, "since that is the case, there is only one thing to do."

"Which is?"

He took a breath. "Eliza, would you marry me? Be my wife, and we can raise this child together?"

When she met his eye, understanding formed between them, the understanding that she had been hoping for.

"Yes, Fitz," she said softly, no longer acting. "I would like that."

He reached out and took her hands within his. "Thank you for understanding."

"I am still cross with you," she said, fixing him a stern look. "I wish you had told me all of this from the beginning."

"It's not an easy thing to discuss."

"But a required one with your future wife. No more misunderstandings, you hear me?"

"Very well," he said. "I will try my best." He wiggled his

eyebrows in a way that would have looked ridiculous on other men, but somehow, he still made it seductive.

"You know, since you are here, we cannot exactly create *more* scandal. Perhaps—"

"No!" she said, getting to her feet. "Have you not learned your lesson, at least the second time?"

"I cannot get you more pregnant."

She rolled her eyes. "Well, *I* have learned my lesson, at least. And not the lessons that you were teaching me. No more experiments. This has gotten me into more trouble than even I can handle."

She walked to the door. The truth was, she was not ready to get any closer to him. He had proven how badly he could hurt her, and she didn't trust him with her heart. Not yet, at least.

"Good night, Fitz."

And with that she left, closing the door behind her. Feeling better, but still unsettled.

She had an inkling that was going to last for some time.

* * *

FITZ BARELY SAW Eliza over the next four weeks leading up to their wedding. She didn't come to him with the news that she had been wrong in her suspicions of expecting a child so she must have been correct in her original assumption – that, or she was playing him. But he had to push that thought aside or it would drive him mad.

With his entire family preparing for their small nuptials, when he asked why Eliza had been avoiding him, she told him that she had been consumed with their preparations.

"I don't understand why it is taking so much planning when we will be the only ones in attendance," he said one night at dinner. "Not that I would mind additional guests, but we do not want to risk that at the moment."

"It is still an occasion to celebrate," Henrietta had said, seemingly aghast that he wouldn't realize that. "We would like to make it a most joyous occasion for both of you."

And so, the day finally arrived, the weather as perfect as could be, the skies clear and the sun shining through. The vicar had agreed to marry them in the small, barely used chapel next to Appleton's orchard. The season was appropriate as the fruit had begun to grow, dotting the landscape in various shades of red and orange.

As he arrived at the chapel, Fitz noticed Eliza standing in a rare moment alone near the front door, staring out over the orchard.

His feet began to move toward her of their own volition and he murmured a quick "excuse me," to Levi before continuing toward her, enjoying watching her as he strolled up behind her.

He thought he had been nearly silent in his approach, but it seemed she had noticed him coming, for she spoke before he could, although she still didn't look back at him.

"This is beautiful," Eliza said wistfully as the wind softly blew back pieces of her hair. "I couldn't ask for a better location."

"What about your choice of groom?" he asked, and she finally turned to him with a smirk.

"He'll do."

"I shouldn't even be seeing you at the moment, I am told," he said. "But I wanted to make sure all was well. That this is what you want. After this, there is no going back."

"I am fairly certain we crossed past that point some time ago," she said, furrowing her brow. "This is about the child now. One which is as real as I ever thought he or she would be."

He nodded, not wanting her to believe he was questioning her once more – not, at least, on their wedding day.

"Of course," he murmured, staring at her for a moment

longer, with so much he wanted to say on the tip of his tongue, words that he couldn't seem to voice.

Instead, he nodded at her and continued within the chapel, a strange sense of melancholy tugging at him. Not because he was marrying her – his intention to do so was certain now. It was because they were doing so with so much unsettled between them.

There was only one way to go now, however.

Forward.

CHAPTER 19

Eliza sat in her bedroom, her wedding nightgown fanned out around her as though she was a prize waiting on a pedestal.

Which, she supposed, she was.

Or she was supposed to be.

Except in this case, Fitz had already received his gift.

Even though she was expecting him, she jumped when the door opened and Fitz stepped in.

"Eliza," he murmured with rare hesitation in his gaze.

"Fitz," she returned.

He slowly stepped into the room toward her, stopping before he came too close.

"How are you?"

She would have laughed were she not so on edge.

"I—" she was about to say that she was well, but that was not true at all. She *had* been well, but now the anxious ball in the pit of her stomach had begun to grow.

It was that same feeling she had when she first realized that she might be expecting, one that came and went but seemed to worsen when she was worried.

As she was right now.

"I am feeling slightly unwell," she admitted.

"I am sorry to hear that," he said, coming to her side and crouching before her. "Is it the baby? Our wedding? The fact that this is our wedding night? I promise, Eliza, that I have no expectations."

"Thank you," she said softly, unable to look at him for a reason she could not name. "Could we simply converse for a time?"

"Of course," he said, taking her hand and helping her stand. "Why do we not sit on the bed where we are more comfortable?"

She nodded before allowing him to lead her over. He fluffed up the pillows, creating a comfortable space for her before leaning her back against them and then taking up position beside her. He didn't touch her, giving her space as he settled one leg over the other and relaxed with his hands crossed over his stomach.

"What would you like to talk about?"

"Our ceremony?" she suggested. "It was beautiful."

"It was," he agreed. "Although no part of it was more beautiful than the bride."

"You are kind," she said, unexpected warmth stealing up her cheeks.

"I only speak the truth."

It *had* been a lovely ceremony. The chapel had been aired out and yet still held a scent of history, of family, of comfort. When she had stepped within, somehow Eliza had known that everything would be all right.

"I—" she began to speak but then a wave of nausea rolled over her and she groaned, shifting so that she was on her side.

"What's wrong?" Fitz asked, immediately kneeling over her, his hands coming to her cheeks.

"I just don't feel well," she said. "It comes and goes but is worse when I don't eat as much as I should. I was so caught up in all that was happening today that I did not have much of an appetite, especially at dinner this evening."

"I noticed," he said, "but I wasn't sure it was my place to say anything."

"You are my husband now," she said wryly. "That gives you the privilege to say whatever you would like to me."

"That may be so, but I am well aware that you are not a woman who would be particularly pleased if I commented on your every movement."

"This is true," she agreed, closing her eyes and breathing in through her nose and out through her mouth as she tried to ease the sensations.

"Can I do anything to help?" he asked, and she nodded slowly.

"I could use something to eat."

"What do you feel like?"

"Pastries," she said. "I always feel like pastries."

"Pastries coming right away," he said, practically bounding to the door, and she cracked open an eye to look at him.

"You're not calling for a servant?"

"I don't trust anyone to select the right ones for you," he said, holding up a finger. "I know where the cook hides her very best."

Eliza couldn't help but smile as he hurriedly left. They had certainly had their misunderstanding, but deep down, he was a good man. She wouldn't have agreed to marry him if he wasn't.

He returned quicker than she expected, but, being Fitz, he hadn't just brought her one pastry. Or even a plate of pastries. No, Fitz had brought her an entire basketful.

"Fitz!" she laughed as she pushed herself up to sit. "Thank you for the food, but I could not possibly eat all that!"

"I can help," he said with a shrug as he flopped down on the bed beside her. "What's your favorite?"

"Do you have a Sally Lunn Bun?"

"I believe I do," he said with a grin. "I was hoping you wouldn't say you wanted the Bath Buns as those are my favorite."

She made a face. "They have currants. Desserts should not have currants."

"That's the very best part!"

He found one for himself and Eliza couldn't help but stare at the sugar crystals that covered it. He noticed the direction of her gaze as he grinned at her.

"You want it, don't you?"

"I don't want the entire bun," she said. "But a bite would do."

Without question, he passed over the pastry and she sunk her teeth into it, scraping off the sugar and the top layer, carefully missing all of the currants, before passing it back to him.

"Thank you," she said from around the pastry.

"You are most welcome," he said, taking a closer inspection. "I see you left me all of the currants."

"Of course. I wouldn't want to deny you the pleasure."

They sat silently for a few minutes, finishing their sweets, before she lay her head back against the pillows.

"Are you feeling better?" he asked.

"My stomach discomfort has eased, but the exhaustion hasn't," she said. "I can hardly imagine how I will feel in a few months if I already need to constantly lie down."

He stretched out on his side next to her, his head resting on his fist.

"I will find the best midwife or accoucheur around – whomever you'd like, in addition to Dot," he said earnestly. "We will make certain that you have the very best care."

"Thank you," she said with a small smile. "I appreciate that. And I am glad that you now believe me."

"I should have from the start," he said gruffly. He reached out and tucked a lock of hair behind her ear. "Go to sleep."

"Do you not want—"

"I want only for you to feel well and stay healthy," he said, shifting his head from side to side. "That is all that matters to me."

"I need to ask you something," she said, tracing embroidery on the gold coverlet with her fingernail. "What are to be the... guidelines of our marriage? I know marriages of the *ton* – especially those that are not based on love – are often marriages only in name. I understand that you did not want to be married so I will not force you into anything, but I feel it best if I know from the start what to expect."

He lifted himself on his elbows and stared deeply into her eyes.

"The beginnings of our marriage may be unconventional," he said, "but there will be no one involved in our marriage except for the two of us. Do you understand?"

"You do not want to take other lovers?" Her heart tripped at the words, but she had to ask.

"No," he said, shaking his head fiercely. "Neither of us will."

She nodded slowly, trying unsuccessfully to hide her emerging smile. She didn't want to appear too eager.

"I would like that," she said softly.

"Good."

She reached a hand toward him and slowly trailed her fingers down his face. "What if I think I would feel better if we were to... enjoy one another and our wedding night?"

His face lit up so intensely that she was nearly blinded. "I think that's a wonderful idea!" He paused. "But only if you feel up to it. And if you would like to stop at any time, that is completely understandable."

She nodded. "I will tell you if I do."

"Thank you."

She leaned in, making the first move.

His words of assurance warmed her heart, filling her with a sense of trust and security that she would never have expected to come from Fitz. It gave her the confidence to meet his lips in what began as a soft, hesitant kiss.

His returning tender touch sent a rush of warmth through her veins, and it was like a spark had been lit and began running along a line of gunpowder to her center, where it exploded in a need for him that overwhelmed all of her other sensations.

His arms wrapped around her, pulling her closer in a deeper embrace as his hands ran gently down her back, sending shivers cascading through her body.

Eliza's mind was awash with a whirlwind of emotions – desire, longing, and a newfound sense of belonging.

They had been together before, but now, joining as husband and wife seemed to hold an entirely new meaning. Every brush of his fingertips against her skin, as he did away with the nightgown that had been designed to easily fall off of her, felt like a revelation, awakening previously hidden sensations.

His kiss was the only place they were currently joined, but he seemed to be interested in changing that as he swept his hand down over the sensitive seam between her legs.

"Are you ready?" he asked, and she nodded against him, returning her lips to his, finding comfort and safety there.

He notched himself against her before slowly easing in, finding home. Her head fell back as she gave in to the sensations coursing through her, and with every subsequent thrust she moaned as she gave herself over to him completely, allowing vulnerability to wash over her.

His thumb circled her nub of nerves as he continued his thrusts, until she unraveled around him, letting herself go, the pulsing waves reminding her of how much she had missed this – missed *him*.

She knew that to give herself to him like this was to open herself up to heartbreak, but he had promised that he would not stray and would remain in her bed and her bed alone. She would have to trust him in that, just as he had eventually trusted her with this baby they had created together.

Even so, she knew that she would have to be careful. She had to shield her heart.

For if she didn't, she could lose everything.

* * *

FITZ COULDN'T SUBDUE the bounce in his step the next morning after leaving Eliza sleeping in bed to begin his day.

"There's the married man," Levi said from the corners of the study when Fitz entered, as he always did, to see to the news of the day before he broke his fast.

"Why are you lurking there in the shadows?" Fitz asked.

"I feel at home here," Levi answered drolly."

"Of course you do," Fitz said with a shrug. Nothing was going to affect him today. He was on top of the world. "Well, what has you hiding in here waiting for me this morning?"

"Siena and I felt it was time for us to return home now that you and Eliza are so… happily married."

"We are married," Fitz said before shrugging quickly. "And I believe that we are happy."

"That's an odd way of phrasing it."

"After last night, I *do* believe that we are happy. Or, at least, we can be."

"So, you are saying your wedding night went well."

"That it did, Levi, that it did," he said with a sigh, taking his seat and leaning back until his feet were high enough to place on the desk, staring at his friend through steepled fingers. He hardly even noticed Levi's scars anymore, he was so used to them, but he knew they must still pain him. It seemed that Siena's presence in his friend's life had helped ease some of his previous uneasiness about them.

A knock at the door signaled Hastings' entrance, which was like clockwork every morning.

"The post has arrived, my lord," the butler said, placing it on Fitz's desk, and Fitz nodded his thanks, although he resolved to ignore it for now.

Until a letter sitting on the top caught his eye.

His name was scrawled across the middle of it in large, thick black handwriting. It was simply handwriting, and yet he couldn't help but consider that it appeared sinister.

"Do you mind if I open just one?" he asked Levi, gesturing to the stack of papers.

"Go ahead."

Fitz sat behind his desk, finding his letter opener before slicing open the seal, one which he didn't recognize.

He unfolded the paper, his heart already racing faster as the words jumped off of the page toward him.

Lord Fitzroy,

I know you believe that hiding in the country will keep you and your family safe. But do not become comfortable, for I will find you, no matter where you hide away. You will have to return to London at some point, will you not? Or else all that you have worked for will come to naught.

And which is worse? To die or to die without a legacy?

It's your choice, my lord.

May the best man win.

The letter fell from his fingers to the desk in front of him, and he looked up in surprise to find that Levi was already there, picking it up and reading it, his senses honed from his years at war.

He looked up sharply at Fitz, who stood in silence, unsure of what exactly he was supposed to do.

"We must go find Hastings and ask where this letter came from," Levi said, already beginning to solve the problem.

"From the post," Fitz said woodenly. "I was so sure that there was no actual threat. That it was over."

"And now you have a wife and a child on the way to think about – not to mention a mother and seven unmarried sisters," Levi said grimly, understanding the gravity of the issue before Fitz himself even did. "This is a serious matter, Fitz, and one that you must address."

"What do I do?"

"You have to make a choice. Do you trust this detective you hired to continue to look into the matter, or do you return to London and see what you can find for yourself? It is someone who has issues with your politics. Who could you have angered to such an extent?"

"A great many people, I suppose, if they knew what I was doing."

"Do many people know?"

"Not that I'm aware of. But you know how people talk."

"Do I ever."

"I will consider my next steps."

"May I make a suggestion?" Levi inquired, to which Fitz nodded. "Ask your wife. See what she has to say about it."

"I do not mind doing so, but Eliza can be… rather reckless. How can I protect her if she will not make the right decision for herself?"

"I suggested that you ask her opinion," Levi said. "You do not need to ask her to *make* the decision."

Fitz nodded. "True."

"I do not think I can leave you with this hanging over your head."

Fitz waved a hand in the air. "Nothing has changed. It is the same threat that has been present since Madeline first tried to poison me. Go. Your wife should be home during her confinement and not in a place where she could be in danger.

I am happy for you and appreciate you spending the last few weeks with us."

"Of course," Levi said with a nod. "You were there for me during trying times, Fitz. Anything you need, just tell me."

"Hopefully nothing untoward will occur," Fitz said. "But if it does, I know where to find you."

CHAPTER 20

The next week was both one of the best and one of the hardest of Eliza's life.

After bidding farewell to Siena and Levi, she spent most of her days relaxing with Fitz's sisters and most of her nights becoming intimate with him – in more ways than just physical. She didn't see him throughout the day for he spent most of it working in his study, but she enjoyed the special winks he would send her way when it was time to meet for dinner or the stolen moments in which he would touch her body or whisper sweet nothings in her ear.

He was so attentive that she nearly forgot there had ever been a time – or two – when she had been angry with him.

All of her belongings had been moved into the lady of the manor's chamber a day after their wedding. It had been vacant, for Fitz's mother had moved to another chamber years ago once Fitz had become Earl. Even so, Eliza felt like something of an interloper, as if she hadn't yet earned her place there.

Fitz had been coming to her so regularly through the door that connected them that when he didn't appear in her bedroom one night, she wasn't certain what to think.

Had he assumed that she needed time away from him? Or had he grown tired of her?

Not one to sit idle and wait for answers, she opened the connecting door, peering around Fitz's room to find that the fire was lit in the grate, Fitz's nightclothes were laid out upon the turned-down bed, but the man himself was nowhere to be found.

Eliza yawned as she stretched her arms, ready to sleep, but first, she would find Fitz to say goodnight.

She knew exactly where he was likely to be – his study, hard at work. For a man who had been so well known for his rakish ways, his dedication was admirable. He must truly believe in his cause.

She tiptoed down the corridor and the stairs, not wanting to wake anyone as the hour was late, which was why she was surprised when she heard voices coming from within the study. Was his mother or one of his sisters not yet abed?

She paused outside the door, not wanting to interrupt their conversation, but then her brow furrowed at the unfamiliar voice.

It was female – low, sultry, and practiced.

"Why are you coming to me with this now?" Fitz asked with irritation in his voice.

"I was afraid before," came the response. "For my life, for the lives of those I work with. I felt threatened. But now... his man keeps returning. Asking where you are, if you have returned. He wouldn't believe that you hadn't been to see us again, as you had been a regular guest for so long."

Eliza's insides turned to ice as she realized just who this woman likely was and what kind of business Fitz had frequented often enough to be known.

"So, finally..."

There was a pause until Fitz spoke in practically a growl. "Finally *what*, Madeline?"

Her response was so low that Eliza nearly didn't hear it. "I told him that you were at your country estate."

"Did you tell him where it was?"

"No," she said quickly. "How could I? I had no idea."

"This is not the entailed estate, so it might be more difficult to find, but it can be located eventually," Fitz said. "Are you ready to tell me just who this man is?"

"Unfortunately, I cannot give you a name," she said. "He didn't come himself. He sent a man in his place to act as a messenger."

"Do you know *his* name?"

"No, but I can describe him."

"Very well," Fitz said with a sigh. "Tell me as best you can, and I will write to the detective."

There was silence but for footsteps that Eliza knew would be Fitz pacing back and forth as the woman was likely doing as he asked.

"You said you didn't know where I was," he said, the footsteps stopping suddenly. "How did you know to come here to Appleton then?"

"I asked one of the footmen at your London house."

"Asked?"

"I… gave him incentive to tell me."

"I see," Fitz said wryly.

"I took the stagecoach here. I will return upon the next one."

"You need to stay the night, don't you?" Fitz said with some resignation.

"I do," she said, the sultriness returning to her voice. "I could stay with you… repay you for giving away information about you."

Eliza's heart leaped from her chest up into her throat. Was he going to take this woman up on her offer? She was experienced and had previously been with Fitz. She could see the draw.

She waited for his answer with bated breath.

"No," he said rather swiftly. "I am married now."

"Are you?" the woman said, humor in her tone. "Congratulations."

"Thank you," he said gruffly.

"You know, marriage doesn't usually keep many of my customers away."

"I have decided to be faithful to my wife," he returned.

Eliza started at that as she considered what he had said and how he had said it. She appreciated that he was not going to go to another woman – but was it because he had no wish to or because he felt that it was the right thing to do? To other women, it might not make a difference, but it certainly did to her.

"Admirable," the woman said flippantly. "Perhaps I could have a bedchamber then?"

"We will find you somewhere," he said. "Perhaps in the dower house. It is not currently in use."

"You don't want to sully your house with me?"

"It's not that," Fitz said. "It's just... my wife is here and I—"

"You do not want her to know of your relations with me."

Eliza decided that she had heard enough. She knew she shouldn't be lurking at doorways, though doing so had certainly revealed her husband's intentions. But she had no wish to listen to herself be discussed.

She took a breath and pushed open the door without knocking.

"His wife is not only in the house but in his room so she would note his absence," Eliza said, placing what she hoped was a confident smile on her face as she assessed the woman who had taken up residence in one of the chairs in front of Fitz.

The visitor was dressed for travel, her cloak of fine fabric, although there was no mistaking the fact that she wasn't a lady, with the long, red corkscrew curls that were allowed to float freely around her head, the rouge that painted her lips and face, and the carefully placed beauty mark above her lip.

"Eliza," Fitz said, the surprise that first crossed his face quickly turning to panic as his gaze flicked back and forth between Eliza and the woman. "My wife, Eliza – Lady Fitzroy. This is Madeline ah—."

"Madeline, how lovely to meet you," Eliza said, taking the chair next to her. Eliza was wearing her nightclothes, but they were all far past that proprietary. "You have news for my husband?"

"How long were you listening?" Fitz asked, leaning back against his desk, disconcerted yet accepting of the circumstance.

"Long enough," she said before turning her attention to Madeline. "I would say that I wished you had come forward sooner, but the time alone together did allow Fitz and me to become remarkably close. However, we could have saved a great deal of tension due to the threat. Although, you know you could have written Fitz a letter. Or even have gone straight to the detective yourself."

"I didn't trust the post or who might come across the letter, and this detective does not seem to be making any progress on your case," Madeline said, her tone sickly sweet. "My only trust was to speak to you myself."

"I do thank you, Madeline. I know this wouldn't have been easy for you," Fitz interjected. "I will compensate you for your travel costs."

"Thank you," Madeline said with a quick nod. "I will return to London tomorrow."

Fitz sat behind his desk, writing something down before passing it to Madeline. "This is the name of the detective. Please reach out to him. I will write to him myself and ask him to make sure that you are protected and not in any danger."

Eliza hated the surge of jealousy that coursed through her. Fitz was only doing what he did best – looking after other people. That didn't mean he was interested in anything further with this woman.

"Thank you," Madeline said, reaching for the letter, and Eliza didn't miss how she allowed her fingers to slowly brush over Fitz's. "If you could see me to the dower house?"

Eliza waited for Fitz's response with raised eyebrows.

"I will ask one of the footmen to do so," Fitz said before grinning. "You seem to have a way with them."

Madeline let out a snort of laughter at that as Fitz called for one of the servants despite the late hour.

Realizing how this would look if the three of them were happened upon, Eliza in her nightclothes, she decided that there was only one thing she could do. Trust Fitz.

"I will wait for you upstairs," she said with a meaningful look at Fitz, to which he nodded.

"Very good. I shall be there shortly," he said, and Eliza forced herself to stand and walk out the door, leaving her husband with an experienced, sensual, beautiful woman – and her trust.

CHAPTER 21

Fitz's step was heavy as he climbed the stairs to his bedchamber after seeing Madeline off into a footman's good hands.

When Hastings had shown her into his study upon her arrival at Appleton, Fitz had nearly fallen over in shock – at her arrival as well as her confidence in walking right in the front door of his family's manor.

But he supposed he had never chosen his companions based on their discretions.

Thankfully Hastings had known that he wouldn't want any of the family to be aware of her presence and had quickly and discreetly shown her into the study.

When Eliza had walked into the room Fitz had nearly walked right out, so unnerved he was by all of the revelations of the evening.

Thankfully, Eliza had seemed fairly understanding of the entire event. He only hoped she would still feel that way when he spoke to her alone.

"Eliza?" he said, wondering why he was always approaching her with such hesitation. He supposed it was because he had never before had a wife, nor even someone he had to answer to. He had always supposed that when he did marry, it would be to a demure woman who wouldn't require an explanation. He could never be certain of what was on Eliza's mind.

"You came," she said, sitting up in the bed, her brows lifting.

"Of course I came," he said, walking over to the bed and taking her hand in his. "You didn't truly believe I would do anything else, did you?"

Suddenly, realization washed over him that this was exactly how she had felt when he had questioned her about her pregnancy – disappointment that no matter what other circumstances had arisen in the past, she wouldn't have faith in him.

"Fitz, if I had any inkling that you might do something I would be disappointed about, I would never have walked out of that room and then welcomed you back here," she said.

"You trusted me?"

"I did," she said with a shrug. "You have given me no reason not to."

The smile began to grow on his face before she held up a finger.

"Now, I can admit that I was not particularly thrilled about searching you out to bid you goodnight only to find you holed up alone with one of your former lovers. But you did soundly reject what she was not so discreetly offering."

"That's her profession," he said. "I suppose she finds it hard to turn it off."

"And you are a hard man to give away."

"That is rather kind of you," he noted.

"I do have a nice side now and then," she smiled at him. "What were you going to say to her before I interrupted you?"

He frowned. "What was I saying?"

"You told her that she couldn't stay in the house because

you had a wife, and then you were about to expand but I walked in."

"Oh," he said, his nose crinkling in the way it did when something troubled him. "I was going to tell her I didn't trust her in the house."

"Because of the staff? There are no other men here. Or were you concerned that she would steal from you?"

"No," he shook his head. "I was concerned that she would try to poison me again."

"What?" Eliza burst out, springing forward toward him. "What is that supposed to mean?"

"She was the one who was paid to poison me, but she stopped me from drinking the poison before it could do anything," he admitted, not seeing any reason to hide the truth from her – until he looked at her face.

She wasn't shocked. She was mad. Raging.

"How could you let her into the house at all?"

"She never meant to hurt me. She—"

"Fitz! She nearly killed you. What if she is here to try again, under the guise of warning you?"

"If she had wanted to kill me, she would have done so by now."

"Unless she had planned to get close to you, and that was why she was trying to seduce you."

The thought had never occurred to him. He would like to think that Eliza was only being overly distrustful, and yet, she had a point.

"Madeline said she is leaving tomorrow and is in the dower house tonight," Fitz said. "All will be well, I'm sure."

"Well, even so, I am not leaving your side tonight."

"You are going to protect me, then?" he said, quirking a brow at her as the dimples broke out on her face.

"That is exactly what I am going to do," she said smartly.

"Well, I place myself into your hands."

"Good," she said. "Now come here. I'll show you just how smart you are to submit to them."

He had no problems in doing exactly as she asked.

Eliza pulled Fitz towards her, heat radiating off her body. He wrapped his arms around her waist, as her heart beat, matching his own rapid pulse. Her hands reached up to tangle in his hair as she pulled him down for a deep, passionate kiss.

Their lips met in a flurry of desire, tongues dancing and exploring. Fitz's hands roamed over the curve of her hips and the swell of her breasts. Eliza moaned softly as Fitz trailed kisses down her neck, nipping at the sensitive skin there before lifting his head to stare down at her, wanting to memorize every detail of her face – the way her eyes sparkled with desire, the curve of her lips as she smiled up at him, the flutter of her lashes against her cheeks.

Eliza reached up, unbuttoning Fitz's shirt slowly. Fitz watched her with a hunger he had never known before. She pushed the shirt off his shoulders, her hands tracing every indent in his abdomen.

"You are so beautiful," she whispered, her voice barely above a breath.

Fitz's emotions surged at her words. No one had ever looked at him with such admiration and tenderness. He leaned down to capture her lips again, their bodies fitting together perfectly as if they were made for each other.

As their passion ignited, their clothing was shed, forgotten in a pile on the floor. Their bodies moved together in rhythm, each touch sending shivers down their spines. Eliza arched beneath him, a symphony of sighs and unintelligible whispers escaping her lips.

Their lovemaking was not just physical; it was a merging of souls, a connection that went beyond anything he could even put into words.

He slid inside of her, finding her more than ready for him.

She was wet and eager, her body welcoming his with a fierce intensity. He thrust into her, a primal urgency driving him. Her gasps only spurred him on, until her muscles contracted around him, her walls tightening, and he knew she was close. He thrust harder, deeper, his own release fast approaching.

As they reached the pinnacle together, her eyes locked onto his, unspoken emotions reaching toward him, reflecting his own back against her.

They fell back on the sheets, lying tangled together, hearts pounding in sync, the warmth of their passion still lingering between them.

Fitz trailed a finger along the curve of Eliza's jawline, trying to take in the moment and commit it to memory. He would never forget this night, the way her skin felt beneath his touch, the way her laugh sounded in his ears. He drew in a deep breath, taking in the scent of her hair, the earthy, sun-warmed fragrance that had been part of his dreams for longer than he'd like to admit.

Hours later, Fitz was still wide awake in the middle of the night, gazing upon his sleeping wife. He gently ran his hand over her soft skin, pausing when he reached her abdomen, where there was the faintest swell that only someone familiar with her body would notice. His child. He placed his palm over her belly, overcome for a moment at the thought that they had made something so special together and that soon enough, there would be a little person in the world relying on him.

Another person.

He had to make sure to be here for the little one, for Eliza, for his sisters and his mother. He had been reckless before, true, but everything he had done in life since then had been for their betterment and their protection.

This threat held over all of their heads had gone on for far too long. What was he to do if they were still in danger when the baby arrived? He couldn't stay here in hiding for the rest of his life. Soon enough, he would be found.

He far preferred that it would happen on his own terms, and not when – or where – it would put those he loved in danger.

He looked down at Eliza, at how peaceful she was in sleep.

There was only one thing to do to keep her safe.

She would hate it. She would possibly hate *him*. But at least nothing would happen to her or their child.

He just had to hope that she would one day understand.

* * *

ELIZA WOKE LANGUIDLY the next morning.

Her stomach was protesting, but when she turned to the side table, she smiled to see that Fitz had left her one of the Sally Lunn Buns she loved so much. She found if she ate before moving she could feel well enough to continue with her day.

She glanced over to the side of the bed where he had slept, the imprint of his head still on the pillow. He had grown so accustomed to sleeping in her bed that she wondered when the last time had been that he had slept within his own.

She didn't mind. She liked being close to him.

He always woke before her, heading down to his study so that he could finish all of his correspondence and send it away so that it would arrive in time for the post to be taken by the mail coach.

It was rather intimate, this living in partnership with another.

Eliza's mother had departed just a few days ago. They had left one another with a tearful farewell, and her mother's promise to return in a few months when Eliza's confinement neared. She would have stayed longer had she not been eager to see Eliza's father, whom Eliza knew she missed desperately. She wondered if that love she had always wanted – the one her parents had – could actually now be within reach. Who could ever have imagined that it might be with Fitz?

Her pastry finished, she donned her slippers and waited for her maid to arrive and help her dress for the morning.

Eliza had a spring in her step, one that had her looking forward to seeing Fitz and wondering if he would have anything to say about their activities last night. They had been even more passionate than usual, she supposed because they had passed the test of trust with Madeline's arrival.

When she finally made her way downstairs and into the breakfast room, she sensed the moment she walked in that something was amiss from the way Fitz's entire family – except Fitz himself, as he was not present – stopped talking and stared at her.

"Good morning," she said, looking around the room, finally stopping on Henrietta's face, which appeared rather pained, quite unusual for her. "Is everyone well?"

"Yes," Fitz's mother finally said, standing with her fingers intertwined. "We must tell you something."

Eliza waited, unable to say anything.

"It seems," his mother began slowly, "that Fitz is... gone."

"Gone." Eliza repeated the word as though by doing so it would make more sense. "Where did he go?"

"It's Fitz," said Georgina, rolling her eyes. "London, obviously."

"Georgie!" Henrietta admonished, elbowing her in the side.

"I'm sorry, but Eliza knows who Fitz is. He had one visit from a working woman and—"

"Georgina Spencer, that is quite enough," her mother said firmly before placing what Eliza was sure was supposed to be a kind hand on her arm. "I am sure that is not the way of it. Fitz is simply being..."

"Stupid," Eliza filled in for her, for she knew exactly what Fitz was doing. "He is trying to get himself killed."

"I would not say that," Lady Fitzroy said, her brow furrowing. "I think he just—"

It seemed that Georgina had more to say about it. "Mother is trying to say that he wanted to return to the excitement of London. That he is bored with being in the country. As we all are. Only, of course, he gets to do as he chooses while we have to sit here with nothing to do, 'just in case.'"

"That's not at all what he is doing," Eliza said, shaking her head woodenly. "He is trying to draw out whoever is after him. To protect us."

She looked around the table at all Fitz's sisters, who sat there staring up at her. The practical Dot. Optimistic Henrietta. Apathetic Sloane. Grumpy Georgina. Even the sickly Sarah and the two youngest, Betsy and Daphne, all wore the same expression. Pity.

"I know what you are all thinking," Eliza said. "That Fitz is bored of *me*. That I am making more of our marriage than what it is. But I know that is not the case. Fitz is worried that whoever is after him has discovered our location. I'm sure he thinks that if he leaves Appleton, he will draw the danger away from us. The only problem is, he is now alone to face his adversary."

It seemed, however, that no one completely believed her, although they were too polite to say so.

"Eliza, why do you not sit and have breakfast?" Henrietta asked, pushing a smile onto her face, but Eliza was suddenly overcome by a bout of nausea and knew that she couldn't stay there a moment longer.

One hand clutching her stomach, the other covering her mouth, she ran from the room as fast as she could before she truly made a fool of herself.

Somehow, she made it all the way upstairs and into her

chamber before she was truly sick, and minutes later, Henrietta came rushing into the room behind her.

"Eliza?" she called out as she stepped through the door and then, seeing Eliza hunched over the chamber pot in the corner, she ran to her, stopping behind her, her arms coming around her. "Oh, Eliza, I'm so sorry."

"It's not your fault," Eliza said, shaking her head. "In fact, there is nothing you can do. I am not upset by what any of you said to me, truly I am not. It is the thought of the danger that Fitz has placed himself in."

Henrietta left her for a moment before returning with a cool, wet piece of linen. "Here," she said, holding it out to her, and Eliza took it gratefully, pressing it to her face.

"Thank you."

"Why do you not lie down for a time?"

"I cannot. I shall rest in the carriage."

"The carriage?" Henrietta said, straightening. "Where are you going?"

"To London. After Fitz."

"Eliza, you cannot go to London!"

"I must. I cannot allow Fitz to be alone."

Henrietta was already shaking her head. "But the very reason he left you was so that you would remain safe."

"True," Eliza agreed. "Which is why I will not go directly to London but rather around it."

"I'm afraid you are speaking in circles I cannot follow."

"I am going to go to the Duke of Dunmore. He will be able to help Fitz. He was trained in war, was he not? Knowing Fitz, he didn't tell the duke that he was even returning to London so Levi wouldn't know that he might need his assistance. I will then remain with Siena so that he feels comfortable in being away from her."

Henrietta paused for a moment before nodding slowly. "Very well. I think I can accept that plan."

Eliza patted her on the arm before smiling at her. "I appreciate your approval, but I am not certain I need it."

"Of course," Henrietta said, biting her lip. "I only want you to be safe. You and the baby. My niece or nephew."

A smile lit her lips, and Eliza had to blink back the tears that were rapidly forming. Goodness, being with child was certainly sending her emotions into turmoil.

"Thank you, Henrietta. We are truly so grateful to have you in our lives."

Henrietta took a quick sniff as well before looking up. "Well. I should probably come with you. You cannot go alone."

"I must, although I do appreciate the offer, Hen. It will be bad enough, however, when Fitz realizes that I have left Appleton. If I bring you into it as well, it will only be made all the worse, and I would feel awful if anything were to happen to you. No. This is my choice, and I will suffer any consequences alone. And Henrietta?"

Her friend appeared troubled, but she was no longer arguing.

"Yes?"

"Please do not tell anyone I am going until after I leave. I know it probably seems stupid of me to go, but I cannot allow Fitz to be alone. The thought fills me with so much apprehension that I know I would be worse off to stay here without him."

Henrietta was staring at her, aghast.

"You love him."

"What?" Eliza started. "We are married. Why would you say that?"

"The way you are talking about him. That fear. A woman only talks like that about someone she loves. I know you both well enough to be aware of why you truly married. It wasn't love then. But it is now."

"No," Eliza said, shaking her head. "I don't—that is I cannot—"

"I know," Henrietta said, placing a hand on her arm. "I can see how Fitz would be both the hardest and easiest man to love. Easy for a sister to love him. Much harder for a woman who is trying to protect her heart."

"That's just the thing," Eliza said, teary-eyed once more. "I am scared. Scared that he might be too reckless, and I would lose him in that way. Scared that he might become bored of me and find another. It's just too much."

Henrietta reached out to her in an embrace.

"You will figure it out. I know you will. Whatever you do, Eliza, though, be safe. Please?"

"Always," Eliza agreed. "Now. If I am going to make it to Greystone in a day, I must leave now. I will see you very soon."

"I will hold you to that. Goodbye, Eliza."

"Goodbye, Hen."

CHAPTER 22

All eyes turned toward Fitz as he entered the House of Lords. They followed him as he walked to his seat in the small room and shifted the heavy weight of his crimson robe over his shoulders. His gaze flickered over to the empty throne sitting at the front of the room as the warmth of the wood paneling, tapestries, and stained-glass windows depicting heraldic symbols and historical scenes washed over him.

He could admit that he had missed it, had missed this – but at the moment, he missed his wife more.

He couldn't help but wonder how she had reacted when she had found out that he had left. Would she have assumed that he had left *her*? That was so far from the case and yet if that was what she needed to believe to keep her safe, then so be it.

Whoever was after him should make their attempt sooner rather than later so this would all come out into the open. He was sick of hiding, sick of the constant worry about those who cared most for him.

He was going to put an end to this. He could practically hear Eliza telling him to do this smartly.

"Lord Fitzroy."

Fitz nearly groaned aloud at Lord Mandrake standing next to him, awaiting his attention.

"Mandrake." He nodded in greeting, not wanting to bother with any further pleasantries.

"I have not heard any response from you regarding my request."

"Your request?"

"I would like permission to court your sister once she returns to London."

Fitz ran a hand through his hair. "Mandrake, I said no."

"Why not?"

"Pardon me?"

"A man deserves to know why his advances are to be rejected, does he not? Your sister could do much worse than a man like me."

"Because... because..." Because Mandrake was a bore. Because he seemed to care far more about his political leanings than he ever could a woman. Leanings that were not at all related to Fitz's.

"I understand that we do not share many viewpoints," Mandrake continued as though reading his thoughts. "But what we do share is the fact that we both want the very best for your sister, and I confess that I am developing feelings of... well, love toward her."

"Love," Fitz repeated, blinking. "You barely know her."

"I know her enough that I respect and admire her more than any other woman. I have met many in my time and never has my heart beaten quite so surely for another."

Fitz had to sit with that for a moment before he could respond. How could Mandrake confess to love his sister when Fitz hardly even knew what he felt for his own wife? Although, from what Mandrake had said, perhaps... just perhaps... he might have some of those feelings himself.

Which was why Mandrake couldn't possibly know if he loved Dot or not.

He couldn't help but realize that perhaps he was being far too stubborn in preventing his sister from receiving the advances of a man she just might actually like. Although if Lord Mandrake was interested... could others who might be a better fit also be forthcoming?

He straightened in his seat when he realized that Mandrake was still standing beside him, awaiting his response.

"I'll tell you what, Mandrake," he said. "If, upon my sister's return to London, she seems interested in spending time with you, then I will allow it. I will warn you, however, that she has not been particularly interested in the courtship of any man in the past."

"You will allow her to decide?"

"I will."

He was not a monster – nor a hypocrite.

"Very good. Thank you, Lord Fitzroy."

With that, Mandrake strode away, heels clicking as he went.

"What was that about?" Fitz turned to find Lord Brighton on the other side of him. Apparently, he had heard the last bit of it.

"Mandrake wants to court Dot."

"You are going to allow it?" Brighton asked with surprise.

"I suppose," Fitz said with a shrug as he began to arrange his belongings, but Brighton was not done with him.

"I hear congratulations are in order," Brighton said, and Fitz noted that a few ears were turned their way. He hadn't read any of the scandal sheets nor heard any of the gossip lately, but he could only imagine that his marriage would have been one of great interest.

"Thank you," he said gruffly, finding that, strangely, he had no wish to speak of Eliza with any of these men, as though he wanted to protect what they had from anyone outside of their lives. "Lady Fitzroy and I are very happy."

Which, he realized, was the truth. He was happy with Eliza, and leaving her had been more difficult than he ever could have imagined.

Brighton had an odd look about him, which Fitz assumed was due to disappointment that Eliza was no longer eligible.

"Cheer up, Brighton," he said, unable to help the jauntiness of his smile. "There are many other lovely young ladies out there. I'm sure one of them will see past your flaws."

He laughed at his jest, but Brighton was not entirely amused.

"Are you happy enough that you are no longer considering this bill of yours?"

"Not at all," Fitz said, shaking his head, knowing that Brighton was a strong supporter. "She is a staunch supporter of mine and the changes I am trying to make."

"Very good," Brighton said, before continuing to his seat as the proceedings of the day began.

Fitz breathed a sigh of relief that Eliza was his and hadn't entertained the idea of any other suitor – the thought of her being married to Brighton or any other man was nearly too much for him to bear.

He shook his head as he considered how much he wanted Eliza to be his and his alone. By all laws and rights, she was.

And yet it meant nothing if she didn't choose him with her heart and her soul.

Now that he had left her, he wondered if he would ever have the chance to make that come true.

* * *

"COME FOR A DRINK WITH US, FITZROY?" Brighton called to him after the proceedings of the day had finally concluded.

Fitz hesitated. He had wanted to check in with his detective to discuss their next plans. He was hoping that they could draw out the person threatening his life by having him be alone somewhere that would be rather tempting, while the detective and his men would lie in wait.

That, however, would take some time to put into place.

"Sure," he said. "Why not?"

It wasn't as though he currently had a wife to go home to, although he found that his desire to stay out late had waned and instead, he simply desired a drink with old friends before returning home to his dreams where he could picture Eliza.

It wasn't long until five or six gentlemen were sitting around a table at White's, Fitz with his usual whiskey in front of him.

"Cheers to Fitz's return," Brighton said, raising his glass up.

Fitz nodded and sipped his drink, the familiar burn racing down his throat into his stomach.

It wasn't as comforting as he remembered, for this was not where he wanted to be. This was not who he wanted to be with.

But it was where he *had* to be, he reminded himself. To protect those he loved.

Which, he realized in a shocking revelation, included his wife.

He had to get this sorted and return to her.

As soon as possible.

It was his last thought as his stomach began to gurgle and his forehead started to sweat. The voices of his friends became distant as the room began to tilt on its side before the world around him faded entirely.

And then everything went black.

* * *

Eliza was exhausted by the time the carriage pulled up at the gates of Greystone.

It had been a longer journey than she had remembered, made even longer by the fact that she was alone.

This was the first time she had ever traveled alone, a freedom she appreciated as a married woman.

It was ironic that when she could finally travel without a chaperone, all she wanted was to be with her husband.

She prayed that he was well, but despite her desperation to see him with her own eyes, she knew better than to go to London herself. Doing so would only put him in more danger.

The duke would help. He had to.

"Eliza!" Siena ran down the front stairs to meet her. "What are you doing here?"

"It's a long story," she replied, accepting Siena's embrace. "One that I'd like to tell Levi as well. Fitz is in trouble."

"In trouble?" Siena repeated, clearly concerned. "Of course. Come in, we shall get you settled."

"There's no time for that," Eliza said, realizing when Levi walked out of the drawing room without a jacket or cravat that she had interrupted Siena and Levi's time together after dinner but there would be plenty of other nights for that.

"Lady Eliza—that is, Lady Fitzroy," Levi said, rubbing a hand over his brow as though he was waking himself up from slumber. "Has Fitz done something to wrong you?"

"No," she said swiftly. "Well, not purposefully."

"I am not certain I like the sounds of that."

"He left Appleton to face his threat."

"He did?" Levi said, his one eyebrow rising above his eyepatch. "Why would he do such a thing?"

"I can only guess as he didn't explain his plans to me," she said somewhat helplessly. "All I know for certain is that he left for London. The rest is all supposition."

"No matter his intention, if he is alone in London, he is in danger," Levi said gravely, confirming her suspicions. "You have come to see if I could help, have you?"

"That's exactly it," she said, nearly sagging into the wall with relief that he understood. "I know you don't want to leave Siena, but if I stayed here with her, could you possibly go to London and ensure that Fitz is well? I hope he at least contacted the detective, but I cannot know for certain."

"Of course," he said. "I shall go shortly."

He crossed over to Siena, wrapping his arms around her and pulling her in closely. Eliza had to blink back tears once more at the affection they showed one another, hoping that she would soon be able to demonstrate to Fitz the depths of her own emotion.

For Henrietta had been right.

She loved him.

Despite all of her intentions to remove her emotions from their physical joining, she couldn't help that she had fallen in love with the way he had cared for her when she wasn't well, how he dedicated himself to his work despite his longing for leisure, and the charming, affable way he approached life.

She could hardly wait to see him again to tell him so.

She just had to believe that there would be the opportunity to do so.

CHAPTER 23

"Eliza? Siena?"

Eliza exchanged a look of unease from across the breakfast table with Siena.

"We're in here!" Siena called out as both of them got to their feet. Levi had only left the night before. Eliza prayed he was returning to tell them that Fitz was fine and, hopefully, had agreed to accompany him here while they made a true plan. The urgency in his voice, however, had her heart beating so rapidly that she imagined it was about to gallop right out of her chest.

Levi pushed into the room, rather disheveled. Eliza realized that her request for him to go to London was a huge one, for despite its proximity to his estate, he had returned to the city only a couple of times since he had been injured. She knew, however, that Fitz was the one person who he would be willing to take the chance to help.

"What is it?" Eliza asked, crossing the room toward him, knowing that she was being rather rude, but she couldn't help herself. She needed the truth immediately. "Where is Fitz?"

"Fitz is… at his townhouse in London."

"Alone?" she insisted, wondering why on earth Levi would have left him there.

"No. I hired another detective to look after him and make sure he is well cared for. A detective who might actually make a difference, unlike the first one. Archibald, I believe his name is."

"Why did *you* hire him and not Fitz?" Eliza asked and, when Levi didn't respond, Siena placed a hand on her husband's arm.

"Why do you not sit down and tell us what you have discovered? I shall pour you some tea."

Levi nodded, taking a seat rather woodenly, running a hand over his face. Eliza retook her chair, trying to be as patient as possible and not demand knowledge on Fitz.

"When I arrived in London, Fitz was already at home," he began, clearing his throat, not looking either of them in the eye. "He had been out at White's with a few other gentlemen. They had just sat down when he had a drink."

He paused, and this time Eliza couldn't help but ask, "And?".

"And then, apparently, he lost consciousness."

"What?" she couldn't help from practically shrieking out, as she jumped out of her chair. "Is he—did he—"

"He is alive," Levi said, reading her thoughts. "But he has not yet awoken."

Eliza felt as though she was going to faint herself – and she was not a woman who had ever been prone to fainting. She fanned her face and immediately sensed Siena at her side, her hands coming under her elbow and shoulder as she guided her back into the chair, placing a cool, damp cloth against her cheek.

"Eliza, take some deep breaths," Siena said, looking over to her husband, who remained as stoic as ever. "Do not forget that you must stay strong for your baby."

"Right," she said, trying to do as Siena said and breathe in through her nose and out through her mouth to hold onto the moment. "Was a physician called?"

"Yes," Levi confirmed. "It was through him that I learned about this detective who is apparently competent and not just out to collect the money of noblemen. The physician assessed Fitz and, from what he can determine, it seems that Fitz was poisoned."

"He should never have gone to London," Eliza whispered.

"I agree," Levi said. "But there is nothing we can do at this point. The physician was able to induce him to vomit which hopefully cleared some of it from his system, but Fitz ingested enough to affect him. Doctor Hudson wasn't certain he could do anymore as we don't know what type of poison it was."

"Could the glass provide a clue?" Eliza said, wrinkling her nose.

"It was gone by the time someone realized what had happened." Levi appeared rather uneasy as though he was trying to determine what to say before he continued, "The rest of the glasses remained on the table, so it is likely that someone purposefully removed Fitz's."

"Whoever he was with likely was the one who poisoned him, then," Eliza breathed.

"Likely, although there were quite a few gentlemen together," Levi said. "The detective is looking into it while the physician told us that all we can do is wait and hope that it clears out on its own and that Fitz will fight to live."

"I must go to him," Eliza said, standing again, causing the footman to step forward, the poor man likely uncertain of just when she would ever make her mind up.

"I agree," Levi said. "I can take you there."

"No," she said, shaking her head. "You should both remain out of harm's way."

"We must make sure that you arrive safely," Siena said softly. "Why do the two of us not ride with you in the carriage to London?"

She looked to Levi, who nodded his agreement.

"Very well," she said, about to advise her maid of their plans before she stopped and looked to Levi once more. "In your opinion, what are the chances that he will be well after this?"

Levi, never one to sweeten the truth, as distressing as it might be, met her gaze and didn't hesitate before he said, "Fifty percent."

"Well," she said, "let's see if we can make that fifty just a little stronger."

* * *

It was truly only a few hours until Eliza was in London at Fitz's – *their* – townhouse, but it seemed like the time had passed interminably.

They walked together into the house so that Levi could check on Fitz once more. As much as Eliza wanted to race to Fitz, she wanted time alone with him and asked Levi to see him first.

Siena sat beside her holding her hand as they waited in chairs outside the room. Eliza tapped her foot worriedly until Levi returned.

She stood, rushing to enter, but he stopped her with a hand on her arm. "Eliza," he said. "I must tell you one thing."

"What is it?"

"The Fitz in that bed does not look like the Fitz you know. But I need you to be strong, and to tell him that you know that he can get through this. Will you do that?"

She nodded woodenly. "Of course."

"Very good," he said. "Thank you for allowing me to see him."

"How could I not?" she said with one last glance to Siena for strength. "Thank you for being here."

Siena let out a slight chortle of disbelief.

"Eliza, you planned my wedding escape! I would do anything for you."

Eliza nodded. "We are there for each other." She took a breath. "Here I go."

The moment she was through the door, she realized why Levi had been trying to prepare her. The Fitz lying in the bed was not the Fitz she knew.

This Fitz appeared sickly, pale, and completely still but for the very slight movement of his chest up and down.

That was the most shocking part of it all.

The Fitz she knew never stopped moving. Even at rest, he was always twitching, touching her, rocking from one side to the other. She had never known Fitz to be so motionless. It unnerved her, and for a moment she couldn't move herself, so caught off guard was she by the Fitz who confronted her.

But he was Fitz. Her Fitz. Still here.

Which was the thought that broke her.

With a sob, she dropped her hands and rushed over to his side, running her hands over his cheeks and down his arms, trying to infuse some life back into his body.

"Fitz," she cried out, her tears finally released as she no longer contained them but instead allowed them to flow freely as she felt everything that had welled up within her for so long. "Fitz," she sobbed, placing her hand on his chest, listening to the slow beat of his heart beneath his ribs and under her ear as she watched his face, completely devoid of emotion or reaction.

"Come back to me," she whispered, turning and cupping his jaw in her hands. "Please. You cannot leave me. Not when I have only just found you. I need you. The baby needs you. And not just because we need you to provide for us. We need you because we love you and I cannot imagine a life without you now. You are happiness and spring and sunshine. You are the spark within my soul and I need you to continue. Do you understand me?"

Her despair fused with anger at the thought of him being taken from her as she reached out and grabbed his shoulders, shaking him slightly, just enough that he moved a bit with her, but not on his own.

"You should never have left Appleton. We knew this would happen, and I am so angry that you would think that putting yourself in harm's way would help any of us. Do you not understand that you and I are part of one another now? That if anything happens to you then I will lose part of myself, for that is what you have become? When we married, we were joined together as man and wife, and I do not want to be without you."

Seeing her words were not working, she leaned forward much more gently, knowing she had lost any control of her emotions but no longer caring. She cupped his face in her hands once more, hating the coldness of his skin beneath her fingertips as she tilted her head forward to rest her forehead against his.

"Come back to me, Fitz," she whispered. "I love you."

She leaned in, and, despite wondering for a moment if she was doing the right thing or had lost all rational thought, she pressed her lips against his.

It was an odd sensation, for the Fitz she knew was never at all passive in his kisses but always the aggressor, giving her all that he had to offer. Even if she initiated any contact, he was always quick to eagerly respond.

She leaned over him, her lips pressed against his, not moving, not seeking anything but connection.

Which was why she was utterly shocked when his lips moved beneath hers.

She pulled back suddenly, wondering if she had imagined it, or if his body had reacted without conscious thought. She stared at him, trying to determine what had just happened – and then screamed aloud when his lips moved.

"What kind of kiss was that?"

His words were gruff and scratchy, as though his vocal cords didn't properly work, but Eliza could not have cared less how he sounded.

"Fitz!" she shouted as she practically jumped on him, tapping his cheeks with her palms, urging him to properly wake up. "Fitz, are you awake?"

"I am now," he mumbled. "Hard for a man to sleep with such an enticing woman lying on top of him."

"My goodness," she said, her sobs beginning afresh, although now they were filled with relief that he had awoken and that there was, above all else, hope.

"What happened?" he croaked out, his eyes opening briefly only for him to squeeze them shut tightly again, likely to hide from the flickering candle beside the bed and the bit of light that peeked in from the windows, which someone – perhaps the physician? – had opened to allow in fresh air from the terrace.

"You were poisoned," she said, swatting him ever so lightly on the arm before changing her reaction and giving him a sip of water instead. "Just as I thought you might be. Oh, Fitz, how could you put yourself through this?"

"Was just trying to protect you," he mumbled, opening his eyes just enough to see her. "Why are you here? You were supposed to stay at Appleton."

"Did you truly think I would remain home and allow you to put yourself in harm's way?" she said crossly. "Who else would have been able to kiss you awake?"

He nodded as though he was considering her question.

"There might have been a lineup at my doorway." Seeing her stare, the corners of his mouth turned upward. "Not that I would ever have entertained the idea of any other woman."

"You better not have," she said before leaning over him. "I know we still have much to get through but I must tell you something – before it's too late."

"You're leaving me? Is the baby not well?

"Why would you say that?" she said, recoiling slightly.

"I need to make sure that it was neither of those things, for both would be the worst news imaginable."

She couldn't help but smile at that, liking what she was hearing.

"I had to tell you that I love you," she said, the words coming out in a rush before she allowed her fear of saying them to overcome her. "You do not have to say it back nor even to return the sentiment. I know that we have made certain aspects of our marriage work rather well and I would like to continue that but do not want anything to be forced. I just wanted you to know… how much you mean to me."

He stared at her unwaveringly. "Did you mean everything that you were saying before?"

"When?"

"Before I woke up."

"You heard that?" she covered her mouth with her hand, absolutely mortified, and he moved his lips into the closest thing to a grin since she had arrived.

"I might have. Something about love, needing me, not being able to live without me… perhaps you should fill in the rest."

"Fitz! How could you not tell me you were awake?"

"I wasn't completely awake. But it's stored in my mind now and will never come out again."

Eliza looked down at her hands, placing them in her lap as she sat perched on the edge of the bed, slightly more ladylike than the initial flinging of herself over his prostrate body.

"Shall we forget I was so… effusive in my words?"

"No," he shook his head, reaching his arms up to her. "Never. That's part of what I love about you. Come here, Eliza."

She blinked. His words had come so fast that she wondered if she had misheard him.

"I-I'm not sure that I can come any closer."

"Oh, you most certainly can," he countered. "Lie right beside me."

She eagerly tucked into his side.

"That's better," he said, nuzzling his nose into the crook of her neck. "Now, I need to tell *you* something."

She waited.

"I love you, Eliza. With all of my heart. For so long, I thought that the woman for me would stand demurely at my side and do all that I requested of her, but I have realized how wrong I was. The woman I need challenges me, makes me better, and ensures that I don't venture off to London alone when there is a threat to my life. I need a woman who can forge her own path forward in life, but who wouldn't want to, for she preferred to have me at her side. I know this baby brought us together. At the time we thought marriage was the only option, but perhaps it just meant that this was the only option for the two of us to be happy."

The tears were back. Eliza found she could hardly take a breath, let alone form any words, so overwhelmed was she by all of Fitz's revelations.

"Could we possibly be this happy together?" she whispered.

"I know we can," he confirmed. "We'd better. It was the very reason I woke up from this."

They laughed slightly at that, as morbid as it was.

"I must go tell Siena and Levi that you are awake," she realized. "They have been so worried."

"Levi's here?" he asked, and Eliza nodded.

"I went to him and asked him to come help you, but we were too late. Perhaps, however, he can help you now."

"If anyone can, it's him."

"I don't want to leave you."

"It's only for a moment," he said. "Besides, Eliza, I need you to know something."

She looked at him expectantly.

"You will never lose me. Even if something did happen to me. Because we will always find one another here." He pointed from his heart to hers. "You are the only one who will ever own mine. And I would like to take up residence in yours."

She nodded, holding her breath, for she had no words – just tears.

But they were happy ones.

For he was right. No matter what happened now, they would always have one another. That's what love truly meant.

CHAPTER 24

*A*s it turned out, devising their trap took much longer than anticipated.

The detective Levi had hired, Matthew Archibald, wanted to be sure that all was in order before they put a plan in place that could cause Fitz to be put in harm's way once more.

Fitz couldn't say that he overly minded, for he spent all of his time with Eliza.

Time which was often spent in bed, after the week it took him to recover.

Eliza refused to leave his side. As much as he wanted her to remain somewhere that he could be sure that she was safe, he supposed if she had to be in London, it was best to keep her close. He loved that she thought she was protecting him, but he supposed, in a way, she was, for her presence encouraged his improvement.

When Archibald came to see him, ready to put their plan into place, Eliza asked to be present in the meeting.

"She insists," Fitz said helplessly as he led the man into his study, where Eliza waited.

Archibald only laughed. "I understand. My wife would do

the same. I am glad to see you on your feet, Fitzroy. When I first met you, you were in a particularly bad way."

"So, I am told," Fitz said, rocking back and forth on his heels. If Eliza's concern hadn't been enough, Levi had come to visit and had told him that he'd had fairly grave concerns that Fitz wasn't going to make it through. Fitz had made a jest of it, telling Levi that he had to change his surly attitude but, deep within, Fitz would admit that he had a similar concern.

If it hadn't been for Eliza, he wasn't sure that he would have been able to have the strength to fight hard enough to return.

But here he was. And he had enough of this.

"I was fortunate that your brother-in-law was summoned," Fitz said. "I hear he is quite an extraordinary physician."

Archibald nodded. "Hudson is certainly sought after, for his patients seem to fare better than most. I agree that you are most fortunate that one of your colleagues knew of his skills."

Fitz paused before they entered the study, a thought striking him.

"Who called him? Which gentleman?"

"Mandrake, I believe his name is."

"Mandrake?" he repeated, furrowing his brow. "Are you certain?"

"Fairly certain, yes," Archibald said as Fitz waved him through the door. "Why does that not seem accurate?"

"Mandrake was who I guessed poisoned me," he said, noting Eliza's look of surprise at his words. "He and I do not agree on anything political, and he was upset with me for my objection to him courting my sister."

"It thought you told him you would allow it," Eliza interjected.

"I said that if Dot agreed, he could call upon her," Fitz said. "That is a far cry from allowing marriage."

"Hmmm," was all Eliza said, as Archibald considered the situation.

"Mandrake was on my list of gentlemen to investigate, but I must tell you that I didn't find anything suspicious about him," he said. "There are two other gentlemen, however, whose actions could be perfectly innocent or could be telling of a crime."

"Who would they be?" Fitz asked, sitting back in his chair, crossing one leg over his other knee. He would have liked to have pulled Eliza into his lap – he had a hard time preventing himself from touching her or drawing her near – but he barely knew Archibald.

"Well, there is Lord Baxter Munroe."

"Lord Baxter?" Eliza exclaimed. "He is my brother!"

"Yes, I know," Archibald said, apology in his tone. "But he has motive, means, and opportunity. I have heard that he was not particularly pleased with the way your marriage came about. Apologies for the directness, but I believe it is suspected that you married in haste due to your... condition, my lady. Munroe was upset about this. Secondly, the apothecary confirmed that he has been a frequent visitor, although he was rather hazy in his memory of what your brother purchased. And finally, he was there at the time of the poisoning and is also a frequent visitor to The Scarlet Rose."

"Madeline's club," Fitz told Eliza, who bristled slightly, but otherwise simply nodded.

"I am well aware," she said dryly.

"Who is your second suspect?"

"Lord Brighton," Archibald said, surprising Fitz.

"Brighton is one of my closest colleagues and an ally in Parliament."

"Perhaps. But I don't believe he is as good of a friend as you might think. He has been speaking with some of the other gentlemen about this bill that you would like to put forward."

"He agrees with me. He is one of my staunchest supporters. Mandrake was one who was opposed."

"Yes, but Brighton would prefer to take the glory for it rather than you. If you were no longer around, then he would have the opportunity to present it and take the credit. Added to that, he was not particularly pleased that you stole Lady Eliza out from under his nose. He has not visited the apothecary, but he does have a small one in his home. It wouldn't take much to achieve what he needed to create a poison."

Fitz was already shaking his head.

"I am not entirely sure what to make of this."

"Which is why we are not coming forward and accusing anyone straightaway. We will have you speak openly about an evening you will partake in at The Scarlet Rose."

"What?" Eliza practically yelped.

"Not to worry. He will not be doing anything there besides waiting to see if someone makes any attempt on his life."

"That's even worse," Eliza said in a more even tone, apparently recognizing that her presence in the meeting wouldn't help matters if she was allowing her emotions to overwhelm all else.

"If we are lucky, we will not even get that far," Archibald said. "I am hoping that this man reaches out to Miss Madeline first and she will tell us of the plans before we have to put anything into place."

"Do we trust her?" Eliza said wryly. "She did try to kill you, Fitz."

"Not entirely," Fitz assured her. "But if she doesn't come forward, then we proceed with the plan as it is. Either way, we will determine who is behind this threat."

"And you will stay safe," Eliza said, staring him down.

"I will," he confirmed.

"Do you promise?"

"I do."

"As do I," Archibald added. "Now, shall we discuss the details?"

"Very well," Fitz said. "Let's finish this."

* * *

MATTHEW ARCHIBALD HAD A FAIRLY sizable number of men working for him, which was both a blessing and a curse.

It reassured Eliza but also meant that it took another week for him to fully assemble his team and ensure all was in place. He had also told them that he wanted to provide enough time for word to spread regarding Fitz's plans to celebrate his recovery.

Eliza was not particularly pleased that Madeline was involved although Fitz seemed to understand her concern.

She sat on the edge of his bed and watched him prepare for the evening in which all was to be set in motion.

He was so handsome that it was difficult to prevent herself from becoming distracted. He had always been strong and well-built, but it seemed to her that his torso and abdomen were even more well-defined than they had been previously. Perhaps it was due to the weight he had lost because of the poisoning and subsequent illness. She would have to ensure that he returned to his full health.

The rosiness had returned to his cheeks and his grin more frequently covered his face.

"Why are you looking at me like that?" he asked, catching her stare in the mirror.

"I find you are all too tempting," she said, walking over to him, catching the edges of his untied cravat and using them to turn him so that he was facing her. She had asked him if she could help him prepare instead of his valet and he had readily agreed.

"Allow me," she said, focusing as she concentrated on her

knot. She hadn't known how to tie one before they had married, but she had loved learning how to do so.

Little did he know, but she was not going to allow him to do this alone.

His mother and sisters had finally returned to London. Initially, Fitz had thought it best that they remain at Appleton, but Archibald had convinced him that he and his men could keep them all safe if they were within the townhouse together, as long as none of them ventured out alone. They had been practically ecstatic, even if they were not yet participating in the events of the season. Hopefully, this would all come to an end soon.

Eliza was most pleased with their arrival, for not only did she have additional company, but she had someone she knew she could convince to aid her in her scheme.

"There," she said, patting the cravat once she had finished. She tilted her head so that it looked straight. "You might have to redo it."

Fitz looked in the mirror and laughed before shaking his head.

"No. I like it just like this."

"It's crooked!"

"You did it. It's perfect."

Eliza's heart swelled as she smiled up at him. He reached out, donning his jacket and securing it before leaning down and kissing her on the lips, bringing his hands to her upper arms.

"I love you more than anything in this world, Eliza. I promise you that we are going to put an end to this threat tonight and that I will keep myself very safe, for I know that is what means most to you."

"It most certainly does," she said. "Do not go back on your word."

"I promise," he said. "Now, allow me to properly kiss you

goodbye and goodnight before we go downstairs and have an audience."

"You think I will be going to sleep in your absence?" she said with a choked laugh. "How could I?"

"You have been rather tired lately."

"Still... I cannot imagine ever sleeping not knowing that you are safe."

"I understand," he said, leaning in and placing a kiss on her forehead. "I love you. Keep that baby safe, all right?"

There was such intent in his eyes that Eliza wondered if there was a chance that he suspected she had her own plans in the works, but he simply kissed her once more before holding out his arm to escort her downstairs, where his family awaited, along with Archibald and a few of the men who would remain for the family's protection.

Eliza took a breath. Soon this would all be over, and they could welcome their child to a happy, threat-free life.

She had to hope that would be true.

CHAPTER 25

"Are you sure this is a good idea?" Dot whispered in Eliza's ear as the carriage pulled up a few businesses down from The Scarlet Rose.

"No," Eliza answered truthfully. "But at least we do have protection."

The carriage door opened to reveal a very wary detective standing on the other side. Mouse, as they called him, had profusely tried to talk them out of this plan, but when he realized that the women were going to go ahead with or without him, he had reluctantly agreed to accompany them.

"I would like to advise you once more to rethink this plan," he said, and Eliza nodded.

"Thank you," she said. "But I believe we will be the judge of that. While I have complete faith that your employer will do everything in his power to ensure that all goes smoothly, no one but women can truly understand the intentions of other women. I do not trust those within the establishment to act in my husband's best interest. That is why we are here."

As she spoke, she waved her hand to Dot, Henrietta, and Sloane, who had accompanied her. Eliza had contemplated asking Georgina but decided that her continual grumbling would only bring them down, so instead, they had snuck out without her noticing.

The man grunted. "Are you certain your husband will be comfortable with your attire?"

"Of course. He will enjoy it," Eliza said confidently, even though she was fairly certain that Fitz would not be pleased that she would wear such a thing out in public. But they had to blend into their surroundings. "Besides, if all goes to plan, he will not even see us. We will stay to the side of the room, observing."

"Very well," the detective said with a sigh before leading them through the door and into the establishment.

Eliza nearly choked as they entered. The room's scent was not unlike that of many ballrooms, only the perfume here was cheaper than she was used to. She supposed it had to do with the fact that she hadn't entered a ballroom for so long, and when she had, she hadn't been carrying a child. Siena had told her that there were a wide variety of symptoms one could feel, enhanced scent being one of them.

One which Eliza was not particularly pleased to have at the moment.

"My goodness," Dot murmured as she looked around the room. She squared her shoulders, appearing rather uncomfortable in her current garments. "I shall find us the best vantage point from which to watch the proceedings."

Eliza nodded, following her as they walked through the gentlemen who surrounded them. She wondered if this had been an appropriate night to choose, for it seemed rather packed. Or perhaps they had all been enticed here by Fitz? He had such an effervescent personality that she was sure men and women alike were inclined to follow where he led.

Once they took a seat, her eyes were immediately drawn to Fitz, despite not even actively seeking him out.

He was standing across the room, speaking to Lord Brighton. Did he truly have ill intent? At the thought, Lord

Mandrake also appeared, at the same time that Dot jolted upright beside her. Eliza followed her gaze to see that she was staring at the marquess with undisguised longing in her eyes.

Interesting.

Eliza leaned to her left to whisper in Henrietta's ear. "Does Dot know that Fitz suspects Lord Mandrake?"

Henrietta met her eye and nodded somberly. "She does. And she's not pleased."

"Hmm," Eliza murmured, wondering what she would do if she was in Dot's position. She supposed all that could be done was to discover the truth.

Eliza's brother was also here, and as his gaze began to swing around the room, Eliza flung out her fan in front of her to hide her face so that he wouldn't see her. The thought of him as a murderer was ludicrous, which was another reason she had decided she had to come herself – to make sure he wasn't falsely accused.

"There's the detective," Dot said, jutting her chin toward Archibald.

"And there," Eliza said, annoyance dripping from her words, "is Madeline."

It was not so much the woman's previous relations with Fitz that annoyed Eliza.

It was that she had tried to kill him, and he had, apparently, forgiven her.

Added to that, Madeline hadn't come forward with any news that she had been approached with a plan to assist in a threat against him. Was it that the attempted killer didn't trust her anymore or had she been convinced to help him?

Fitz nonchalantly placed his drink on the table beside him. Eliza knew the plan. The detectives were watching closely to see if anyone tampered with it, although Eliza doubted anyone would do so out in the open.

It was the second part of the plan she most hated – as did Fitz. He would enter a private room, allegedly with a woman.

The previous attempts had been made on his life when he was alone, so it only made sense that was when he would be most under threat again.

After a few moments, nothing untoward occurred, although Eliza's gaze was caught by a feminine figure meandering through the crowd, her attention on Fitz. Eliza stood, bracing herself, ready to run after the woman if she attempted anything.

"Eliza!" Henrietta yanked her down. "What are you doing?"

"That woman over there," she pointed across the bar. "She is watching Fitz."

"Are you going to chase after her and knock her out of the way with your body?" Henrietta asked, waving to Eliza's stomach.

Eliza had done her very best to disguise her condition with her choice of garments, and while she was certain she had succeeded, she appeared slightly more ample and was far too tired to chase after the other woman.

But she had determination on her side.

"Yes, as a matter of fact, that is exactly what I was going to do."

"If you see a threat, tell our escort," Henrietta said, pointing to the detective who had accompanied them and was now leaning against the wall with his arms crossed over his chest, not exactly blending in, in Eliza's opinion.

"Very well," Eliza grumbled, looking up to find Fitz, only to discover to her horror that while she and Henrietta had been talking, he had disappeared.

And so had the woman who had been watching him.

"He's gone!" Eliza exclaimed.

"Who is gone?" Dot asked, her eyes still on Lord Mandrake.

"Fitz!" Eliza said, annoyed as she felt that Lord Mandrake could wait. Fitz was the one currently in danger. "Where did he go?"

She stood and turned to their escort. "Mr. Mouse, we must find Fitz."

He shook his head, looking troubled as he pushed himself away from the wall. "Call me Mouse. That is not my job. I am here to protect you. This place is full of men on the watch for him. I'm sure he hasn't gotten far."

"Do you think he was taken to the private room?" Eliza asked Henrietta, who seemed to be the only reliable one among them. Sloane's eyes were hooded as she continued to gaze about the room.

"We must assume this is all part of the plan," Henrietta said, although her overly optimistic attitude was not much help at the moment.

"I am sorry, Hen, but we must assume the worst and hope for the best. We have to find this room." She looked to Dot and Sloane. "Why do the two of you not stay here and keep an eye out for him in case he returns?"

"Lady Fitzroy, I cannot allow you to separate from one another," Mouse said, looking pained.

"Not to worry, I will be with them."

Eliza turned at the familiar voice and nearly sagged in relief to find Levi standing there. "Oh, Your Grace, I am so happy to see you. Where is Fitz?"

"I am trying to determine that myself," he said in a gravelly voice. "But first, please tell me you did not bring my wife along with you."

"I did not," Eliza said, despite the momentary pang of guilt at knowing what Siena would think at being left behind. "I didn't want to put her at risk, not in her condition."

"A condition in which you find yourself as well?" he said, quirking his eyebrow.

"Fair point. But this is my husband we are talking about. I could hardly sit at home and—"

"Allow men who do this professionally to take care of it?"

"Exactly," she beamed before remembering how dire their situation was. "But we can concern ourselves with that later. We must worry about Fitz now. Did he go to one of the back rooms?"

"Yes, but Archibald is with him."

"Who accompanied them?"

"Madeline."

Eliza narrowed her eyes. "I don't trust her."

"Lady Fitzroy, I understand, but—"

"It is not the history," Eliza said firmly, shaking her head. "Call it women's intuition. Something is amiss. I am certain of it. I hope I am wrong, but I cannot take that chance."

Levi sighed. "Very well. Come with me."

Eliza and Henrietta followed him along the side of the dark corridor, Henrietta hiking up her dress, which threatened to fall below her bosom.

Eliza's breasts were pushed up far higher and plumper than ever before, her pregnancy helping them up.

"I believe it's the second door on the right," Levi said, pointing to a short corridor. "Archibald is hiding within the room."

"Is there another entrance?" Eliza asked, and Levi furrowed his brow.

"Not that I am aware of."

"We best check," she said, glancing furtively around. "There is a detective guarding this door. I am sure the man at the end of the hall is one of them. We should go around to the other side."

She could tell Levi wanted to argue but she was grateful that he allowed her to do as she wished while he followed along behind. They turned the corner and Eliza stopped so suddenly that Henrietta ran into the back of her.

"What is it?" Henrietta hissed.

"There she is," Eliza whispered over her shoulder as she gestured behind her so that they could hide around the corner. She peered around the wall. "The woman that I noticed earlier. She's entering another room."

Levi looked around. "It appears to be the room beside the one Fitz is in."

"Could there be a connecting door between them?"

"Why would the detectives not know about that?"

"Who gave them the layout?" she asked pointedly before rolling her eyes. Men. This was why she'd had to come.

"I think she is going to enter from the other side."

Sure enough, the woman stepped forward, knocking softly on the door, and moments later it was opened. The woman pushed through the door, entering almost silently, and every hair on Eliza's body seemed to be standing on end as she was certain that all was not well here.

It was then she noted that the door had been left open a touch.

"That's it," she said, lifting her heavy skirts in both hands. "I've had enough."

"Eliza, you could ruin the plan," Henrietta said, but her words were not about to stop Eliza.

Nothing could.

Except for the man who reached out to grab her the moment her fingers touched the doorknob.

CHAPTER 26

◈

Something didn't feel right.

Fitz had hoped to avoid this night in the first place. He had been certain that Madeline would come forward and tell them of any plans she had been approached with.

But unfortunately, nothing had come to fruition and here they were.

His skin crawled just from being here, as if his body knew that it should be at home with Eliza instead of within such an establishment, even if his mind knew his true purpose, which was to bring this to a finish in order to protect her.

He had noted that all of the suspects were here – Baxter, Brighton, and even Mandrake, who he still considered as the person who would have most reason to want to do away with him.

He recognized all of the detectives situated around the gaming hell and had been sure to place his drink in opportune positions to invite poisoning multiple times.

When nothing occurred, Archibald's second man, Pip, signalled him to enter the private room. Fitz had leaned over to Madeline to tell her that it was time to move to the next step in their plan. She had nodded in apparent delight before leading him down the corridor to the agreed-upon room where Archibald was waiting, hidden behind a heavy curtain in the corner.

Fitz stepped in, surprised that the room which at one time in his life had seemed a haven away from the rest of the world now caused him nothing but discomfort. Archibald was so well hidden that even Fitz, who knew he was there, couldn't see him.

"What do we do now?" he asked the room itself. "Wait?"

"I believe that is the plan," Madeline answered him, even though she had not been the one to whom he was directing his question.

"No one reached out to you, Madeline?" he asked, crossing his arms over his chest as he studied her, recalling Eliza's words.

"No," she said, shaking her head, although she was looking at the candle she was lighting and not at him. "Not directly."

Fitz's nerves were on edge. He couldn't say why, but all was not right.

"Archibald?' he called out. "Are you still here?"

When silence met him, he stood and began to pace across the room, flicking back the curtain where Archibald was supposed to be.

He wasn't there.

At least, he wasn't standing there.

Fitz's heart began pounding even harder when he found the detective lying prostrate on the floor.

He didn't have time to check if he was still breathing, for he heard the all-too-familiar sound of a click behind him as a pistol was readied to fire. He whirled around, only to find Madeline standing there with a gun in her hand, pointed directly at him.

Her hand was shaking, and while that told him that she

wasn't completely comfortable with what she was doing, he also knew that a gun was often never more dangerous than in the hands of a scared holder.

He held his hands up in front of him. "Madeline," he said slowly, trying to reason with her. "What are you doing?"

"I'm sorry, Fitz," she said, true regret in her eyes. "I wanted to say no, but he upped the amount he offered. I couldn't turn it down."

"Who is *he*?"

"The—the gentleman that I told you about."

As she spoke, a curtain across the room moved, and what had been a hidden door opened, revealing another woman he didn't recognize.

"Who are you?" Madeline demanded, her eyes flicking over to her in fear.

Madeline's concern did not bode well for Fitz.

"I am here in case you cannot do the job," the other woman said, her eyes cold and glittering. Fitz knew he might have been able to talk Madeline out of this, but he was certain this other woman would be much more determined to finish the job. Finish him.

"He didn't trust me?" Madeline said indignantly.

"You do not seem to be a person that anyone should trust," Fitz couldn't help but remark, although that didn't seem to help matters, for it only caused Madeline's hand to become slightly steadier when she pointed the gun at him.

Fitz sighed. Eliza had been right. He *would* have reminded himself to always trust her in the future, except he had a feeling that he wasn't going to have much of a future after this. If Archibald was down, Fitz didn't want to think about what that meant for the rest of the men who were standing in wait.

Madeline must have shared the part of the plan that she had been aware of with his adversary, but Fitz could only hope that she had been kept in the dark enough that some of the detectives could maintain their disguises.

His eyes kept flicking to the door, waiting for one of them to enter.

To his great relief, just as it seemed the second woman narrowed her eyes, likely about to pull her trigger, the door pushed open.

Only, it wasn't one of the detectives who entered.

It was Eliza.

Fitz's mouth dropped open as he forgot, for a moment, where they were and what was happening.

All he could focus on was her beauty, her courage – and, he would admit, the way her breasts were nearly popping out of the most scandalous gown he had ever seen.

Then he remembered that the entire reason he had put this plan into place was to ensure her safety, and here she was, right amid the chaos and two guns, one which was pointed at him and the other at her.

"I knew it!" she crowed as she glared at the women who threatened him. "Take your guns off of my husband!"

Fitz didn't think he had ever loved her more.

* * *

ELIZA'S MOMENT of panic at being caught had quickly diminished when the hands that had grabbed her dropped just as fast. Levi had come to the rescue.

The man certainly knew how to fight. She supposed years at war would do that.

She was never more grateful for her friend's choice of husband than at that moment. She had barely blinked by the time Levi had wrestled the man off of her and to the ground.

"Lord Brighton," she muttered in disgust, nudging him with her toe before she returned her attention to Levi. "What did you do to him?"

"A simple trick I learned years ago. He's asleep but he will wake up soon enough," Levi said. "We best act fast."

Eliza nodded as Levi bent, whipping off his cravat and using it to fasten the man's hands behind him. Eliza, however, didn't have time to wait as she pushed open the door and stepped into the room.

It was heavily scented in musky fragrances, with sweeping, jeweled-toned curtains surrounding the room. The bed was placed in the center of it all. She was nearly sick right where she stood at the thought of Fitz here with any of these women, but that was the past, she reminded herself. Their future was together.

All that fled from her mind, for there was Fitz, caught in the center of the room beside the bed, two pistols trained upon him by women on either side.

"I knew it!" she couldn't help but exclaim at Madeline's role in all of this, although she appeared rather uncertain. "Take your guns off of my husband!"

"I can't," Madeline said in just over a whisper, her eyes flicking to Eliza for a moment. "You don't understand."

Remembering what Fitz had told her about Madeline, her daughter, and her need to provide for her, Eliza took a small step toward her, more compassion filling her than she would have thought when it was towards a woman who currently held a gun aimed at her husband. "I understand that you are only doing what you feel is best for your family, but I can assure you that your daughter is far better with you in her life than as an orphan after her mother is hanged for murder."

Madeline began blinking rapidly as her eyes filled with tears.

"That is easy for you to say. You have no idea what it is like to be within my circumstances."

"You are right. I don't," Eliza said, hating that her heart did feel for this woman, as, no matter how dire her own situation might have felt, Eliza had always known that she would have someone to look after her. If not Fitz, then her father or her brother. This woman could only rely on one person and one person alone – herself.

"There are people who would help you if you'd let us. Fitz would. I would."

"It's too late," Madeline said in a shaky voice. "He'll kill me."

"No, he won't," Levi said from behind Madeline. "He is rather... incapacitated at the moment."

"I think you are all forgetting something," the woman from across the room interjected. "*I* have nothing to lose. I have no daughter to worry about, no cares in the world at all. I am not threatened by you, nor is the man who hired us, for you cannot prove anything."

She walked over toward Fitz, but her eyes were on Levi. She began shaking her head.

"I wouldn't try that, if I were you, Duke of Death. Oh, yes, I have heard about you. You might be quite the shot, but you best leave that pistol where it belongs, or I will kill your friend here before you can even remove it from your waistband. Some of us can be just as good of a shot without the benefit of war, did you know that? If the army would have taken me, they would have had quite the asset, let me assure you."

"You're Lady Danger," Madeline breathed out from where she stood across the room, her own pistol lowered, at least. "I have heard of you."

"Heard of me, perhaps," the woman said smugly. "Most who *see* my face once do not live to see it again."

Eliza's heart beat fast. If Madeline and Levi were scared of this woman, then what chance did it leave any of them?

Eliza locked eyes with Fitz, who was ignoring them all as he continued to stare at her.

"I love you," he mouthed toward her, and her eyes

widened as she realized that he had given up – that he was going to give *himself* up – likely to save her.

"No," she shook her head as she cried out the words, ready to launch herself toward him – just as the small dagger went sailing by her, right toward Fitz.

* * *

FITZ KNEW when he heard the words "Lady Danger" that there was no way they were all getting out of this alive. The woman was known throughout England for her prowess. A hired assassin, one who had been taking the papers by storm, for she was unable to be caught by even the best detectives in the land.

There was only one way out – by sacrificing himself. He was who she wanted. If he could distract her long enough, Levi should be able to take care of her and save the rest of them.

As she reached her left hand behind her and closed it around something that he knew would be another weapon, he leaped forward to take her down with him – but when he went flying forward into the air, he landed with an "oof" on the sofa bed before him as the dagger went sailing over his head and landed with a thud in the wall behind him.

He scrambled to his feet to ensure that Eliza was well, only to first see Archibald, tying the hands of Lady Danger behind her.

"Archibald," he said in relief. "I thought you were dead."

"Fortunately, I have a hard head," the detective said, rubbing a spot on the back of his head, his hand coming away red when he dropped it. "It was sufficient, however, to knock me out long enough."

He looked around the room. "Is everyone well?"

Eliza stared back at him with an expression of disbelief as

Levi was currently occupied with divesting Madeline of her pistol.

Then Henrietta's face appeared around the doorway, and Fitz groaned aloud.

"How many of you came?" he asked, his relief fleeting at concern that they had all put themselves in danger.

"Dot and Sloane are here too," Henrietta said. "But they were with Mouse in front."

"Is it over?" he asked, looking at Levi, who nodded slowly, his good eye fixed upon him.

"I hope so," he said. "It appears Brighton was the one behind this all."

"Brighton?" Fitz repeated, surprised. "I didn't think he had it in him, truly."

"There will be much to discuss," Archibald said. "But I think we would all prefer to do it in your drawing room rather than in the middle of this hell or brothel or whatever you call this place. Lady Danger will be coming with me, but as for Brighton and Miss Madeline. Their fates are up to you."

Fitz looked over at Madeline, who appeared near to collapsing.

"Eliza?" he asked his wife. He wanted to have mercy on Madeline, but he wouldn't if it would make Eliza uncomfortable. She was the one who now mattered most.

She crossed the room, stopping in front of Madeline, who appeared wary. Eliza reached out, surprising them all by taking her bound hands in her grasp.

"You will take your daughter and you will leave this city," she said firmly yet, strangely, kindly. "My issue with you is that you have now threatened my husband's life twice, and I cannot sleep well knowing that you are nearby, perhaps willing to do so again. If you leave us be, then I have no issue in seeing you go free without charge. You obviously care deeply for your daughter, and I have no wish to see a child motherless."

Madeline nodded slowly. "Thank you. I can do that." She looked from Eliza to Fitz and back again. "I am truly sorry."

Fitz rocked back and forth. He hadn't cared as much when he was the only one in danger, but now that Eliza was part of it...

"I am not certain how truly sorry you are, Madeline, or else you would never have taken such an action a second time. You are lucky, however, that my wife has a forgiving heart."

Eliza shook her head, not denying his words but also not taking the credit.

"I cannot see how, as a woman who is going to become a mother soon myself, I could advocate to take away the mother of another child," she said. "But I do have to consider my own family and safety. I can only hope that all of this is behind us now."

Madeline, her face pale, nodded and began to slip out of the room as though she was worried that they might change their minds – which was a valid concern.

Fitz had no problems letting her go.

"Eliza?" he said, turning to his wife. "Let's get out of here."

"Gladly," she said, smiling as she took a step toward him.

He couldn't wait to wrap his arms around her and show her how much he had missed her, even if it had just been for a few hours. He needed to revel in the feelings of relief and safety once more. The look on her face told him that she felt the same, but just as they took a step toward one another, concern flashed over her eyes.

She stopped for a brief moment before crumpling forward – his heart sinking to the ground along with her.

CHAPTER 27

Fitz rushed forward, catching Eliza just before she hit the floor.

"Eliza!" he called out, cradling her face in his hands, desperate for her to respond as Henrietta crowded next to him. He looked wildly around him as Dot and Sloane soon joined them. Word had gotten out that all had been taken care of back here and it seemed the room was practically flooded with detectives – detectives who they could have used a few minutes ago, although that was not his primary concern at the moment.

"What's wrong with her?" he asked Dot, who quickly knelt beside them, easing Eliza down so that her head was in Fitz's lap.

"It's hard to tell and we are not exactly in the best place to assess her," she said. "Her breathing is easy, however, and she doesn't appear to be in any distress. I guess that she was simply overwhelmed, but let's get her home."

Archibald passed them, leading out Lady Danger. "I'll have Hudson come to your townhouse, Fitzroy."

"Are you sure you wouldn't like him to take a look at your head first?"

"I'll be fine. He can see me after. It's handy having a brother-in-law for a physician."

Fitz nodded, although he didn't have it within him to engage in such a conversation at the moment – not when he wasn't sure if Eliza was well.

Henrietta led them through the door to the connecting room, then through to the back of the building. Here, at least, the air was less suffocating than it had been within and, fortunately, the ladies' carriage was nearby.

The detective who accompanied them – one whom Fitz could not blame, for he knew what it was like dealing with his sisters – helped him settle Eliza within for what was, thankfully, a short drive home.

Fitz sat on one side of the carriage, Eliza lying before him with her head in his lap while the others crowded on the other side. Eliza had curled into him as though they were cuddling in bed.

He kept an arm around her, holding her close, while Dot placed a hand on her forehead and inspected her as best she could in their surroundings.

"I suspect that the excitement of the evening overcame her," Dot said. "But we will be sure all is well, Fitz, don't worry."

He nodded, even though he couldn't say anything, for his throat was far too tight.

Soon enough, they made it home and he carried Eliza inside, passing by the waiting servants without a word until he could lay her down on the sofa in the front parlor.

"If everyone could stay back except Fitz?" Dot asked as she examined Eliza, scaring Fitz when she even looked beneath her skirts.

"Just to make sure there is no bleeding," she murmured, which nearly had Fitz losing consciousness himself at the thought.

Dot opened a vial from a bag that one of the maids had

brought at her request and waved it before Eliza's nose as Fitz waited breathlessly. After a moment, Eliza began to stir, and Fitz was immediately in front of her face, needing her to awaken.

"Eliza?" he called out before patting her cheeks. "Eliza!"

"Fitz," she said, a caress in her voice as she slowly blinked her eyes open. "You are well. Thank goodness."

"*I* am well?" he said, nearly choking back a laugh. "Eliza, you fainted!"

She pushed herself up, with Fitz and Dot helping her until she was leaning back against the sofa cushions. Fitz quickly rectified that by taking a seat next to her and holding her against him.

"I am home," she said, looking around her, the simple expression causing Fitz's entire body to warm.

"Yes," he said, "home. You're home. With me."

"How do you feel?" Dot asked. "Your cheeks are slightly pink. I expect the exertions of the day overwhelmed you, did they not?"

"I think so," Eliza said as she took a deep breath, blinking. "How did I get here?"

"In the carriage," Fitz said, trying to be patient. "What do you think happened?" he asked Dot as the door opened and the physician – Hudson – walked in with his medical bag.

"The physician might know better than I, but I did notice that you didn't eat much at dinner, Eliza," she said without judgment.

"I couldn't," she said. "Not with the anticipation of tonight."

"Between not eating enough, the many emotions that you must have felt tonight at the club, and the heat of the room, it was all likely too much," Dot said. "Good evening, Doctor Hudson."

"Good evening, everyone," he said, before kneeling in front of Eliza. "I hear we had a fainting spell."

"I wouldn't call it a fainting spell," she said, nearly indignantly. "I have never fainted in my life."

"Well, we shall call it a pregnancy-related episode, then," he said. "I would guess that your sister-in-law is correct, however. It is good to see you, Lady Dot."

"You know one another?" Fitz asked, looking back and forth between them.

"I do. Your sister has been instrumental in a few of the births I have attended," the physician said. "She is very good at what she does."

Fitz knew that Dot would excel at anything she chose, but he had no idea to what extent she had accomplished her work.

"Now, let's have a quick look at you," he said as Dot kindly yet firmly pulled Fitz back and away. He reluctantly followed her, although he wasn't entirely pleased about it.

He stood as close as he could, arms crossed over his chest as he watched the physician with Eliza. It wasn't long until Hudson stepped back before explaining his thoughts, addressing all of them.

"Lady Dot is, I believe, correct," he said. "My best advice is to try to keep your life as calm as possible until the baby arrives. Can you do that?"

"I sincerely hope so," she said, and Fitz nodded.

"I promise it will be so," he said. "Whatever she needs."

"I'm glad to hear it," the physician said. "If you need me for anything at all, you know where to find me. In the meantime, I will be off to see to my brother-in-law."

"I imagine that is not for the first time," Fitz said wryly.

"Not at all," Hudson laughed. "The man is forever getting himself into one scrape or another. If not on the job, then at home."

"At home?" Eliza asked.

"Let's just say that his wife has a propensity for taking in every stray animal she has ever laid eyes on. Not all are as friendly as they should be."

"I see," Eliza said, even though she still seemed curious. Before she could ask more questions, however, it was time she rested.

"Thank you, Doctor," Fitz said, shaking the man's hand. "We appreciate all that you do."

He walked him to the door, giving him a generous payment before returning to Eliza.

"Now," he said. "You have had quite the day. Best get you to bed."

She pushed herself up to a sitting position, but before she could start walking upstairs, Fitz bent down and scooped her up in his arms.

"Fitz!" She laughed. "What are you doing?"

"What I should have done a long time ago," he grunted. "Used brute force to take you where you are supposed to be."

"I am perfectly fine to walk," she said, even as she snuggled her head into his shoulder.

"That may be so, but you will have your every need looked after for the rest of this pregnancy, understand?"

"Very well," she said, looking up at him with a smile.

When he made it to the top of the stairs, he took her right into his bedroom, lying her down on the slightly bigger bed.

"I need to prepare for bed," she said. "My maid will be waiting."

"I shall tell her that she can retire for the night," Fitz returned. "I will be taking care of you."

He did so as gently and tenderly as he could, lying her down and removing all of her garments before helping her to don her nightgown, wiping her face, her hands, and tucking her into the blankets.

"Will you lie with me?" she asked, holding her hands toward him.

"Of course."

He huddled in under the covers with her, wrapping his arms around her and pulling her in close against him.

"You scared me today," he murmured.

"You scared me!"

"Let's keep things... boring from now on, shall we?" Fitz said, brushing tendrils of hair back away from her face.

"Boring sounds good to me," she said, her eyes already closing.

Fitz placed a kiss against her temple, drew her in against him, and soon they both fell asleep, wrapped up in their love for one another.

* * *

"Well," Fitz said from his place at the head of the table the next morning. "I can finally say that all is well. We are out of danger, and we can all resume our lives as we please."

Eliza smiled at him from her place next to him, as Fitz reached over and squeezed her thigh beneath the table.

"Wonderful," Lady Fitzroy said from her place at the opposite end. "Now we can return to society and find husbands for all of you."

Georgiana and Sloane both groaned aloud, while Dot appeared rather speculative.

"Since we now know that Lord Mandrake is not threatening our family, have you allowed him to call upon me?" she asked, and Eliza followed her gaze to Fitz, who fidgeted rather uncomfortably.

"If that is what you want, Dot, then so be it."

"Thank you," she said shyly before looking down at the table before her. Eliza could hardly imagine what she could see in a man as boring as Lord Mandrake, but if he made Dot happy, then so be it.

"Wonderful," Lady Fitzroy beamed. "As for the rest of you, I already have a list of potential suitors prepared."

"Mother, I'm not entirely sure that we are interested in any of the suitors that you have in mind, let alone them being interested in us," Sloane said pointedly, actually joining in the conversation for once.

"Nonsense," her mother said, shooing her words away. "Now that Fitz is married, I'm sure we are seen as a particularly suitable family."

Eliza had to swallow her choked laughter at that. While she was hardly a woman who would lead to suitability, she would do all she could to help Fitz's sisters – but only if that was what they wanted.

"Anything you need," she murmured.

"Very good," Lady Fitzroy beamed before Henrietta spoke up.

"There is something that has troubled me," she said. "If Lord Brighton was interested in seeing you killed or too ill for Parliament, why did he not try anything when he visited us at Appleton?"

"Archibald asked him that, actually," Fitz said. "He wouldn't answer, but according to Madeline, he didn't dare to try anything himself. He was happy to pay someone else but didn't have the stomach to go through with it with his own hands."

"I believe that's even worse," Eliza mused, and Fitz nodded.

"Exactly."

"What will happen to him?" Dot asked.

"He will go before the House of Lords, who will decide his fate," Fitz said. "I will warn you that the trial will likely attract a great deal of notoriety, but we shall stay as quiet about it as possible. I would assume that he will likely be exiled or imprisoned, but we will find out in due time."

Eliza couldn't help but shudder.

"What about your bill?" she asked.

"I will send it forward when all of the talk dies down," he

said. "I wouldn't want this scandal to overshadow what I am trying to do."

"Well," Eliza said, looking at him admiringly. "I am proud of you, Fitz."

"We all are," his mother added, and, even though it was breakfast, he lifted his cup of tea.

"To the most wonderful women in the world, who have allowed me to be the man I am. I am grateful for you all."

As they clinked their glasses together, Eliza couldn't help but reflect on how lucky she was to have found a family just as loving as the one she had come from.

She would be forever grateful that she had found her happily ever after.

EPILOGUE

SIX MONTHS LATER

Fitz paced back and forth in front of Eliza's bedroom door. "It's been too long, hasn't it?" he asked Georgina, who was seated across from him, one hand on her chin.

He was well aware that she had been tasked with keeping an eye on him while his mother, Eliza's mother, Dot, Sloane, and Henrietta were in with Eliza and the physician, although Georgina hadn't hidden her disdain for the job.

"Childbirth takes some time, Fitz," Georgina said, rolling her eyes at him. "You have to be patient."

"I am not a patient man."

"I hadn't noticed."

He shot a look her way at her sarcastic tone.

"I'm concerned for her."

"I know," she said, softening. "I can understand how you would be ill at ease due to the sounds coming from that room."

"Georgie!"

"It's the truth," she said with a shrug.

At the next cry from within, he stood, stomping over to the door.

"That's it. I'm going in."

"I don't think men are supposed to go in there," she called after him, but he was not to be deterred.

He stopped in shock at the sight before him, hating the look on Eliza's face. He rushed over to her, practically knocking Henrietta out of the way to take her hand.

"Eliza," he said, holding her hands against his chest. "I'm here."

She squeezed his hand so tightly that he nearly cried out in pain himself, and Henrietta sent him a smug "I-told-you-so" look as she backed away, cradling her own.

"The baby's coming," Dot said from her position at the end of the bed, and Fitz watched, eyes wide, as his son slipped into the world in a feat of great strength from Eliza.

Moments later, the baby cried out, and Fitz's jaw opened in shock that a human – one he had helped create – was in front of him.

As Dot cleaned the baby with a piece of linen, Fitz leaned down and placed kisses all over Eliza's face, wiping the tears that fell from her eyes when she opened her arms and accepted the baby.

Fitz sat down next to her, his arms drawing around her.

He wasn't sure what he had done to deserve this – the most amazing woman in the world as his wife, a healthy baby in her arms, family surrounding him, and growing support for his proposition – but he would accept it with all of the gratefulness in the world.

"I love you, Eliza," he whispered in her ear before kissing her once more.

"And I love you, Fitz," she said, tilting her tear-stained face toward him. "I always will."

"It's our happily ever after," he said.

"It is," she said, with a watery smile. "And the best part about it is that we are just getting started."

* * *

Dear reader,

I hope you enjoyed Fitz and Eliza's story! I had so much fun with the two of them and would love to know what you thought! You are always welcome to email me at ellie@elliestclair.com, post in my facebook group or, of course, leave a review.

Wondering what might happen with Dot and Mandrake? Their story, Her Honorable Viscount, will be coming soon. In the meantime, if you love some mystery sprinkled in with your romance and haven't yet read my Remingtons of the Regency series, then be sure to start with The Mystery of the Debonair Duke!

If you haven't yet signed up for my newsletter, I would love to have you join us! You will receive a free book as well as links to giveaways, sales, new releases, and stories about my coffee addiction, my struggle to keep my plants alive, and how much trouble one loveable wolf-lookalike dog can get into.

www.elliestclair.com/ellies-newsletter

Or you can join my Facebook group, Ellie St. Clair's Ever Afters, and stay in touch daily.

Until next time, happy reading!

With love,

Ellie

Her Honorable Viscount
Noble Pursuits Book 3

SHE BREAKS ALL CONVENTIONS. He follows every rule. How can he trust his love at first sight?

HER HONORABLE VISCOUNT - A SNIPPET

"Hurry, Miss, she needs you quickly."

Dot followed the shadowy figure down the alleyway, her eyes flicking from side to side for signs of danger.

She was committed to her work, but that didn't mean she was interested in risking her life.

She had to be smart. Cunning. Outwit both those who might guess her true identity and those who might discover her secret one.

"This way," the man in the heavy cloak said, ushering her through a small doorway and into the tiny house, heavy with the scents and sounds of childbirth.

"Sally, midwife's here. Hold on."

Dot rushed into the room, as proud and surprised as ever that the announcement of a midwife meant *her*.

"There, now, let's see how we're doing," she said, kneeling beside the woman's head and cupping her cheek to comfort her before moving lower to check the baby's progress. "Look at that, we're not far."

Dot worked with another woman in the room, who quickly introduced herself as a sister. A mere hour later, the baby emerged, and Dot united mother and baby, ensuring all was well.

The proud father, who had fetched her and led her here not long before, entered the room, all smiles as Dot faded into the background, cleaning up to allow the family their time together.

Her heart was full seeing their smiles and the unity they shared. This was why she did what she did. She loved every moment of the process, from helping women when they first heard the joyous news until the baby was settled in their arms.

She wasn't naïve. Not every situation was a happy one, and yet she was also pleased to be there to help a woman in a troubling situation or to provide comfort when needed.

No one else understood it – most certainly not her family.

But at least they wanted to see her happy – even if it meant she undertook a profession that could ruin their family.

The only problem was that she wasn't certain she would ever have what the women in her care did, not when her station in life was so far removed from her purpose.

But that was a worry for another day.

Some of her midwifery visits stretched to even days at times. However, this one being so short meant that the hour was early enough that there were still people out in the streets but late enough that most of those were coming home from taverns or other rather unsavory endeavors. She should have listened to her brother and brought a groom along, but she had wanted to avoid burdening any of the servants with what could be a long night without sleep.

She wasn't about to pull this man away from his family to accompany her home, and when she bid them all farewell, they barely even noticed her, so caught up were they in their newfound joy.

With a small smile and her supply bag in her arms, Dot

slipped out the door, wrapping her cloak around her head, hoping she would pass for someone of far lesser status than she was. She had purchased the cloak in a market near here and far from Mayfair in the hopes that she would blend in, as most of the families she served were those who needed help but didn't have the means to afford a usual midwife or physician to attend to them.

She hurried down the alley, hoping to make it to her brother's home unnoticed. She pulled up quickly when she saw a group of men huddled around a door, backtracking when one of them turned and noticed her.

"'Oy! You there!" one called out to her, taking a step forward, but Dot was already turning around and running in the other direction, her heartbeat quickening.

She was sure she could handle herself if the situation called for it. She had a dagger in her pocket and a fair bit of knowledge on combatting a foe in her head.

If it was ever discovered who she was, however… that was where the real danger lay.

Footsteps resounded behind her, heavy and increasing in speed, and Dot broke into a run, no longer attempting the pretense that she wasn't aware of who was following her.

Her shoulder was caught from behind, and she fought it, hoping she could outrun her pursuers or at least find a haven somewhere, but she was still a fair way from such a destination.

Suddenly, so quickly that she couldn't avoid him, a tall figure stepped out of a doorway and into her path. She stumbled into the man, her arms reaching out to brace her fall. Dimly, she noted that the fabric of his jacket beneath her fingers was quite fine, but before the fact could truly register, she heard the click of a pistol, and her breath caught.

"I suggest you all back away. Now," the steely voice bit out.

Dot turned around, seeing the men who had been chasing her raise their arms and begin backing away.

"No problem 'ere, just wanted a word," the more vocal man said. "Off we go now."

As Dot turned back to her savior, she knew she should be wary. The dismissal of a pack of men for another stranger in the dark within this neighborhood didn't necessarily mean safety.

Only, as she looked up – quite a ways up – recognition She knew this voice. She knew those eyes. She knew this man.

Mandrake.

Preorder Her Honorable Viscount on Amazon!

ALSO BY ELLIE ST. CLAIR

Noble Pursuits
Her Runaway Duke
Her Daring Earl
Her Honorable Viscount

Reckless Rogues
The Duke's Treasure (prequel)
The Earls's Secret
The Viscount's Code
The Scholar's Key
The Lord's Compass
The Heir's Fortune

The Remingtons of the Regency
The Mystery of the Debonair Duke
The Secret of the Dashing Detective
The Clue of the Brilliant Bastard
The Quest of the Reclusive Rogue

The Remingtons of the Regency Box Set

The Unconventional Ladies
Lady of Mystery
Lady of Fortune
Lady of Providence
Lady of Charade

The Unconventional Ladies Box Set

To the Time of the Highlanders
A Time to Wed
A Time to Love
A Time to Dream

Thieves of Desire
The Art of Stealing a Duke's Heart
A Jewel for the Taking
A Prize Worth Fighting For
Gambling for the Lost Lord's Love
Romance of a Robbery

Thieves of Desire Box Set

The Bluestocking Scandals
Designs on a Duke
Inventing the Viscount
Discovering the Baron
The Valet Experiment
Writing the Rake
Risking the Detective
A Noble Excavation
A Gentleman of Mystery

The Bluestocking Scandals Box Set: Books 1-4
The Bluestocking Scandals Box Set: Books 5-8

Blooming Brides
A Duke for Daisy
A Marquess for Marigold
An Earl for Iris
A Viscount for Violet

The Blooming Brides Box Set: Books 1-4

Happily Ever After
The Duke She Wished For
Someday Her Duke Will Come
Once Upon a Duke's Dream
He's a Duke, But I Love Him
Loved by the Viscount
Because the Earl Loved Me

Happily Ever After Box Set Books 1-3
Happily Ever After Box Set Books 4-6

The Victorian Highlanders
Duncan's Christmas - (prequel)
Callum's Vow
Finlay's Duty
Adam's Call
Roderick's Purpose
Peggy's Love

The Victorian Highlanders Box Set Books 1-5

Searching Hearts
Duke of Christmas (prequel)
Quest of Honor
Clue of Affection
Hearts of Trust
Hope of Romance
Promise of Redemption

Searching Hearts Box Set (Books 1-5)

Christmas

Christmastide with His Countess

Her Christmas Wish

Merry Misrule

A Match Made at Christmas

A Match Made in Winter

Standalones

Always Your Love

The Stormswept Stowaway

A Touch of Temptation

Regency Summer Nights Box Set

Regency Romance Series Starter Box Set

For a full list of all of Ellie's books, please see www.elliestclair.com/books.

ABOUT THE AUTHOR

Ellie St. Clair is the creative mind behind Regency romances featuring strong, unconventional heroines and men who can't help but fall in love with them. Her novels perfectly blend passion, mystery, and suspense, transporting readers to a world where love conquers all, even the darkest secrets.

When she's not weaving tales of love and intrigue, Ellie can be found spending quality time with her husband, their children, and their beloved dog, Bear, a spirited husky cross. Despite her busy life, she still finds joy in the simple pleasures—whether it's savoring a scoop of her favorite ice cream, tending to her garden, or challenging herself in the gym. An avid plant enthusiast, she's on a never-ending quest to keep her indoor greenery thriving.

She also loves corresponding with readers, so be sure to contact her!

www.elliestclair.com
ellie@elliestclair.com

- facebook.com/elliestclairauthor
- x.com/ellie_stclair
- instagram.com/elliestclairauthor
- amazon.com/author/elliestclair
- goodreads.com/elliestclair
- bookbub.com/authors/elliest.clair
- pinterest.com/elliestclair

www.ingramcontent.com/pod-product-compliance
Ingram Content Group UK Ltd.
Pitfield, Milton Keynes, MK11 3LW, UK
UKHW031336180225
4646UKWH00009B/19